NEW YORK REVIEW BOOKS
CLASSICS

SÃO BERNARDO

GRACILIANO RAMOS (1892–1953) was born and raised in the northeastern Brazilian state of Alagoas, where most of his books are set. He moved to Rio de Janeiro as a young man to work as a journalist but returned home a few years later to start a family and, following his father, run a general store. In 1928, he was elected mayor of his town, Palmeira dos Índios. He was initially reluctant to assume the post—his predecessor had been shot—but under pressure from a powerful local family, he gave in, promptly passing anticorruption laws. One of his unusually vivid municipal reports made its way into the press and caught the eye of the poet and publisher Augusto Frederico Schmidt, who contacted Ramos to ask if he was writing anything else. He was: his first novel, *Caetés*, was published shortly thereafter to acclaim. Ramos would go on to publish three more novels, as well as children's books, short-story collections, and two memoirs. He also translated Booker T. Washington's *Up from Slavery* and Albert Camus's *The Plague* into Portuguese. Between 1936 and 1937 Ramos was jailed by the government of the dictator Getúlio Vargas on suspicion of participating in a communist revolt. (He joined the Communist Party years after his release.) His memoir of his imprisonment was published in 1953, the year he died of lung cancer.

PADMA VISWANATHAN's novels, *The Toss of a Lemon* and *The Ever After of Ashwin Rao*, have been published in eight countries and short-listed for numerous prizes. Her fiction, journalism, personal essays, reviews, and translations have been published in *Granta*, *Boston Review*, *Brick*, *Two Lines*, and elsewhere. Canadian by birth, she is an associate professor of creative writing at the University of Arkansas in Fayetteville.

SÃO BERNARDO

GRACILIANO RAMOS

Translated from the Portuguese by
PADMA VISWANATHAN

NEW YORK REVIEW BOOKS

New York

THIS IS A NEW YORK REVIEW BOOK
PUBLISHED BY THE NEW YORK REVIEW OF BOOKS
435 Hudson Street, New York, NY 10014
www.nyrb.com

Published by arrangement with Literarische Agentur Mertin Inh, Nicole Wit, e.K
Frankfurt am Main, Germany.

MINISTÉRIO DA CIDADANIA
Fundação BIBLIOTECA NACIONAL

MINISTÉRIO DA
CIDADANIA

MINISTÉRIO DAS
RELAÇÕES EXTERIORES

PÁTRIA AMADA
BRASIL
GOVERNO FEDERAL

*Obra publicada com o apoio do Ministério das Relações Exteriores do Brasil em
cooperação com a Fundação Biblioteca Nacional.*
Published with the support of Brazil's Ministry of Foreign Affairs in cooperation with
Brazil's National Library Foundation.

Library of Congress Cataloging-in-Publication Data
Names: Ramos, Graciliano, 1892–1953, author. | Viswanathan, Padma, 1968–
    translator.
Title: São Bernardo / by Graciliano Ramos ; translated by Padma Viswanathan.
Other titles: São Bernardo. English
Description: New York : New York Review Books, 2019. | Series: New York Review
    Books Classics | English translation of Brazilian novel. | Identifiers: LCCN
    2019017357 (print) | LCCN 2019018920 (ebook) | ISBN 9781681373867 (epub) |
    ISBN 9781681373850 (paperback)
Subjects: | BISAC: FICTION / Crime.
Classification: LCC PQ9697.R254 (ebook) | LCC PQ9697.R254 S213 2019 (print) |
    DDC 869.3/41—dc23
LC record available at https://lccn.loc.gov/2019017357

ISBN 978-1-68137-385-0
Available as an electronic book; ISBN 978-1-68137-386-7

Printed in the United States of America on acid-free paper.
10 9 8 7 6 5 4 3 2 1

CONTENTS

I

BEFORE I started this book, I thought division of labor was the way to go.

I approached several friends, and most of them heartily agreed to pitch in for the betterment of our national literature. Padre Silvestre would look after the moral side and the Latin quotations. João Nogueira took on punctuation, spelling, and syntax. I promised Arquimedes the typography, while for literary flair I invited Lúcio Gomes de Azevedo Gondim, editor and director of the *Cruzeiro*. I'd outline the plan, insert the basics of agriculture and cattle-raising, cover the costs, and put my name on the cover.

It was an exciting week, meeting with my main collaborators. I could already see the volumes on display, one thousand sold thanks to the eulogies I'd placed in the wafer-thin *Gazeta* on Costa Brito's recent death, trying to gain some advantage. Anyway, my optimism went up in smoke when I realized we weren't all seeing eye to eye.

João Nogueira wanted a novel in the language of Camões, with sentences turned back to front. Count me out.

Padre Silvestre gave me a chilly reception. After the October Revolution, he turned fanatical, demanding rigorous investigations and punishments for anyone who wouldn't wear a red scarf. He gave me the side-eye. And we were friends! Those patriots. It's fine—everyone has their obsessions.

I dropped him from the plan and set my hopes on Lúcio Gomes de Azevedo Gondim, a good-natured journalist who writes what he's told to.

We worked for a few days. Afternoons, Azevedo Gondim would leave the newspaper to Arquimedes, lock the nickel-and-dime drawer, and pedal his bicycle out to São Bernardo, half an hour on the roadway that Casimiro Lopes had been trying to fix with a couple of other guys. He'd comment on the day's headlines, denounce the government, drink the glass of brandy Maria das Dores brought him, and, feeling important, meekly command, "Let's get to it."

We'd go to the porch, sink into wicker chairs and work out the plot, smoking, looking out on the Caracu heifers grazing in the pasture below and farther out, at the edge of the woods, the red roof of the sawmill.

At the start, everything went well. We were in perfect agreement, had long conversations. But each of us turned out to be listening to himself, not taking seriously what the other said. Warming to my subject, I forgot what Gondim was actually like. I saw him as some kind of blank page receiving the confused ideas boiling up in my brain.

The result was a disaster. Two weeks or so after our first meeting, the *Cruzeiro*'s editor presented me with two typed chapters of nonsense. I lost my temper. "Go to hell, Gondim. You've made a mess of the whole thing. It's pompous, it's fake, it's idiotic. No one talks this way!"

Azevedo Gondim switched off his smile, swallowed the insult, and swept together the shards of his meager vanity. Sulking, he objected that an artist can't write the way he talks.

"He can't?" I asked, astonished. "Why not?"

"He can't because he can't," Azevedo Gondim replied.

"It's like this because it's always been that way. Literature is literature, Sr. Paulo. Folks argue or fight, go about their business in a natural sort of way, but arranging words color-fully is something else. If I wrote the way I talk, no one would read me."

I got up and leaned on the balustrade to get a closer look at the Limousin bull Marciano was leading into the cowshed. A cicada started buzzing. Old Margarida was coming along the wall of the dam, bent double. In the church tower an owl hooted. I shuddered, thinking of Madalena, and filled my pipe. "It's the devil's own job, Gondim. It's all gone to pot. Three failed attempts in a month! Drink your brandy, Gondim."

2

I ABANDONED the project, until one day I heard another owl hoot. All of a sudden, I started writing, relying on my own resources and not worrying about whether it would benefit me, directly or indirectly.

Ultimately, it was just as well that Padre Silvestre, João Nogueira, and Gondim didn't cooperate. There are matters I wouldn't reveal face-to-face to anyone. I'll describe them here because this book will come out under a pen name. Of course, if anyone knew I wrote it, they'd call me a liar.

Let's continue. I mean to tell my story. It's tough. I might neglect to mention useful details, ones that seem to me beside the point, irrelevant. Or maybe, more used to dealing with hicks, I won't trust readers to understand and will repeat insignificant passages. All the rest of it will be arranged without any order, as you'll see. It doesn't make any difference. As my mestizos would say, there's more than one way to skin a cat.

Seated here at the dining table, smoking a pipe and drinking coffee, I sometimes pause this slow work, look out at the orange-tree leaves darkened by night, and say to myself, A pen is a heavy object. I'm not used to thinking. I get up and go to the window that looks out onto the vegetable garden. Casimiro Lopes asks if I need anything.

"No."

Casimiro Lopes squats in a corner. I return to my seat and reread my cheaply made sentences.

Look. If I'd had half of Madalena's education, I'd burn through this. Now I recognize some value in that pile of papers. As far as book learning goes, I'm pretty well-versed in statistics, cattle-raising, agriculture, commercial accounts—all useless for this kind of writing. If I resorted to all that, I'd come off as an egghead, throwing around technical expressions the average guy would never know. Apart from all that, though, I'm totally ignorant. And clearly, at fifty, I'm not about to learn anything new.

I didn't learn the rest when I was young, because I wasn't interested—I was pointed in another direction. My goal in life was to take possession of the lands of São Bernardo, to build this house, to plant cotton and castor beans, to put up the lumber mill and the cotton gin, to organize these tangled woods into orchards and chicken runs, to put together a proper herd of cattle. All this looks easy when it's done and summed up in a couple of lines, but for the guy who's trying to get started, peering in every corner to figure out what to take hold of, it's terribly hard. There's also the chapel, which I built because of Padre Silvestre's hints.

Being busy with these enterprises, I never tried for João Nogueira's learning or Gondim's rot. Readers will therefore be so kind as to translate this into literary language if they want to. If they don't, no great loss. I'm not planning to play the writer—too late for a change of career. And that little boy crying over there needs someone to keep him on the straight and narrow, someone to teach him the rules of living well.

"So what are you writing for?"

"No idea!"

The worst part is I've already wasted several pages and haven't even started yet.

"Maria das Dores, another cup of coffee."

Two chapters gone. Maybe, with edits, I could use some of Gondim's pages after all.

3

LET ME start by declaring that my name is Paulo Honório, I weigh eighty-nine kilos, and I turned fifty on São Pedro's day. The age, the weight, the bushy gray eyebrows, and this whiskery red face have brought me quite a bit of respect. I got less respect before acquiring these features.

Frankly, I use São Pedro's day and that year because they're in the parish book of baptism registrations. I have a certificate mentioning godparents but no father or mother. They probably had their reasons for not wanting to be identified. So I can't celebrate my birthday precisely. In any case, if there's a discrepancy, it's probably not big—a month, give or take. Doesn't matter: we don't have exact dates for lots of important events.

So I'm the first of a family line. On the one hand, that might not sound like a happy condition, but on the other it means I don't have any poor relatives to support, those shameless nuisances you usually find slithering alongside people working their way up.

If I tried to tell you about my childhood, I'd have to lie. My guess is I drifted around. I remember a blind man who used to pull on my ears and old Margarida, who sold sweets. The blind man disappeared. Old Margarida lives here at São Bernardo, in a clean little house. She doesn't bother anyone—costs me ten milreis a week, hardly enough to pay her back for everything she gave me. She's lived a century, and one of these days I'll buy her a shroud and bury her near the high altar in the chapel.

Until I was eighteen, I hoed a hard row, earning five tostões for twelve hours' work. That was when I committed my first act worthy of mention. At a wake that ended up in a free-for-all, I moved in on this girl Germana—a *sarará*, a blond mulatta, flirty as hell—and tweaked the stern of her ass. The kid about wet herself, she loved it so much. Then she flipped and made up to João Fagundes, a guy who changed his name so he could steal horses. The upshot was that I knocked Germana around and knifed João Fagundes. So the police chief arrested me. I was beaten with a bullwhip, took my medicine and stewed in my own juices, rotting in jail for three years, nine months, and fifteen days, where I learned to read with Joaquim the shoemaker, who had one of those tiny Bibles, the Protestant kind.

Joaquim the shoemaker died and Germana was ruined. When I got out, she'd gone downhill—had an open-door policy and the clap.

By that time, I wasn't thinking about her anymore, though. I was thinking about making money. I registered to vote, and Sr. Pereira, a moneylender and political boss, loaned me one hundred milreis at five percent interest a month. I paid back the hundred milreis, and took two hundred with the interest cut down to three and a half percent. He never went lower than that, and I studied math so as not to be robbed any more than suited me.

Like a beast at the gelder's (to put it crudely), I thrashed in Pereira's claws. He sapped me muscles and nerves, the scum. I got my revenge afterward: he mortgaged his property to me and I took it all, left him in his breechcloth. But that was later on.

At first, capital kept giving me the slip though I chased it nonstop, traveling the backlands, trading in hammocks, livestock, pictures, rosaries, knickknacks, winning some here, losing out there, working on credit, signing notes, carrying out extremely complicated operations. I went hungry and thirsty, slept in the dry sand of riverbeds, fought people who only spoke in shouts, and sealed commercial transactions with loaded guns. Here's an example: Sr. Sampaio agreed to buy a herd of cattle from me, but when push came to shove he gave me the cold shoulder and stood around picking his teeth. I went back and forth, around the bend, trying to get him to pay up, but he was hard as nails. I cried to him about my miserable luck: I had a bushel of debt, this was no way to deal with people, so on and so forth, etc. This barefaced cheat, a big gun in his town, a mover and shaker, he told me off. I wasn't discouraged: I picked out a few fellows from Cancalancó, and when the gentleman headed back to his ranch, I jumped him, tied him up, and dragged him into the scrub, tearing his hide on the cactus thorns— prickly pear, mandacaru, xique-xique, and foxtail.

"Now let's see who's got clothes in the rucksack. I'll show you how many logs it takes to make a canoe."

The gentleman—who could have taught weasels a thing or two—rattled on about justice and religion.

"What justice?" said I. "There's no justice and there's no religion. What there is, sir, is that you're going to cough up thirty contos and six months' interest. Pay up or I'll have you bled, nice and slow."

Sr. Sampaio wrote a note to his family and delivered

thirty-six contos and change that same day. Casimiro Lopes was the courier. I gave him a receipt, thanked him, and said goodbye. "Thank you. God bless. Adieu. I truly regret having inconvenienced you. And don't come after me with your justice, because if I see you, sir, I'll turn into a rabid dog and you'll die on a blunt knife."

I didn't appear again in those parts. If I had, I would have been rifle-shot for certain, my face skinned and unrecognizable, my teeth bared and grimacing at the sun, fortune gone. For safety, I used to carry my money inside a big cowbell corked with leaves and hung on my saddlebow. If the money and leaves ever fell out, the bell rang.

Eventually, I tired of that gypsy life and returned to the woods. Casimiro Lopes, who knows enough to stick to what he knows, came with me. I like him. He's brave, he lassos, he tracks. He's got a dog's nose and a dog's devotion.

4

I DECIDED to plant myself here, where I'm from—the town of Viçosa, in Alagoas—and before long was planning to buy São Bernardo, the property where I'd worked the fields for a five-tostão wage.

My old boss, Salustiano Padilha, penny-pinched his whole life to make his son a doctor, then wound up dying of ulcers and hunger without seeing anyone in his family get the degree of his dreams. Acting like I didn't want anything, I tried to run into Padilha's son, Luís. I found him in a pool hall, soused, playing baccarat. Now, it's true that you can make a living, however crummy, from that game, but a guy who plays drunk has no judgment. I hung around the table for a half hour: a greenhorn, he was getting taken.

I got friendly with him and within two months loaned him two contos that he frittered away fast—on card games, parties with salt cod and cane liquor, and strumpets at the Breadless Crust. Watching all this idiocy made me pretty confident. When he came one day, broke again, and invited me to a São João's party at the ranch, I released another five hundred milreis, pretending to be uninterested in the IOU. "What's this for? Between us? Formalities . . ."

But I hung on to that paper.

The property was falling to pieces: brushwood, mud, rove

beetles like the devil. The manor house walls were crumbling and the roads nearly impassable. But what excellent land!

That night, the blacks raised dust, dancing samba in a blowout in the main room. The band, bass drum and flutes, played the national anthem, while Padilha wandered out to the spiderweed-infested courtyard with a bunch of mestizas to do twirls around a bubbling pot of *canjica*. I pulled him away from this very interesting pastime.

"Why don't you cultivate São Bernardo?"

"How's that?" Padilha asked, rubbing his eyes because of the smoke and leaning against a papaya tree that was wilting in the heat of the fire.

"Tractors, plows, proper agriculture. Ever thought of it? How much do you think this place would bring in if a person made good use of it?"

Luís Padilha, with hand and lip, indicated his pitiful ignorance as a property owner. He returned to the mestizas and the dancing I'd interrupted, without even seriously considering the matter. But in the wee hours, he badgered me—plastered, moaning incoherently, raising his head at each jolt of the oxcart taking us to the city. "So rich, Sr. Paulo. Gonna be a run of bad luck." He grabbed hold of one of the oxcart posts and focused on vomiting. Afterward he snoozed, only to wake up miserable and belching. "Plows. There's nothing like plows."

He came to see me the next day, still bearing traces of his binge.

"Sr. Paulo Honório, I've come to consult you. You, sir, a practical man—"

"At your service."

"I believe I already told you that I've made up my mind to cultivate the ranch."

"More or less."

"I've made up my mind. The way it is now won't do. It produces plenty, but it could produce so much more. With plows ... Don't you think so, sir? I'm thinking of a manioc plantation and a flour mill, modern. What do you say?"

Asinine. Spoiling land this fertile by planting manioc! "Good idea."

I didn't pay any more attention to the matter, just left him to get worked up, hashing out his project in the Gurganema at night to the sound of a guitar. He really transformed himself. Waving around a bottle of cachaça on the stone banks of the Paraíba River, he annoyed his drinking buddies, ranting about seeds and chemical fertilizers. He got more and more big-headed, wanting to learn agronomy. Before long, the whole city knew about the crops, the machines, the flour mill.

"How's the farming coming along, Padilha?"

At first he answered, until he realized they were mocking him and started avoiding people, wounded by his friends' treachery.

"Savages!" he snarled, letting himself be cheated at baccarat. "Get off it."

Folks never knew whether he was talking about the table-mates fleecing him or the pals pulling his leg. He sought me out and vented. "Savages! It's a major enterprise, as you can see, sir, and these jackasses are picking on me. Around here, no one understands anything, Sr. Paulo. This is one sad place. Around here, the only things they take seriously are double-dealing and underhandedness."

Full of bitterness and wavering on his earlier decision, he confessed that he'd tried to get a loan from Pereira. "The ninny! I made a comprehensive presentation, thoroughly demonstrated that it's a magnificent project. He didn't believe me, said he was strapped. So I thought maybe you might be interested in this opportunity. Think you might want to shell out about twenty contos?"

Smiling, I looked closer at this wee yellow beast, with his thin lips and rotting teeth. "Hey, Padilha," I said jokingly, "you ever roll your own cigarettes?"

Padilha said he bought his cigarettes ready-made.

"More convenient, I agree, but also more expensive. So, Padilha, if you rolled your own, you'd know how hard it is to roll a thousand. Now imagine how much more work it is earning one milreis than rolling one cigarette. One conto is made of a thousand milreis bills. Twenty contos is twenty thousand milreis. You make it seem like you don't know all this, talking about twenty contos that way, making that face as if money was dirty paper. Money is money."

Padilha hung his head and muttered peevishly that he knew how to count. He left, but he kept coming back, insisting.

"Am I a capitalist, man?" he griped. "You want to wipe me out?" Then he offered me a mortgage on São Bernardo.

"Bunkum. São Bernardo isn't worth a parrot's breakfast. Pereira's right. Your father let the property go to seed." In the end, I promised vaguely, "All right. I'll think about it."

The next day, I was still thinking about it. "We'll see, Padilha. Money is money."

I spent a week playing this game, collecting information about old Mendonça's age, health, and finances. When I made my decision, wise men swore I was crazy.

Padilha got the twenty contos (less what he owed me, with interest), bought a printing press, and started the *Viçosa Mail*, an independent political newspaper that had a run of only four issues before it was replaced by the Literary and Recreational Guild. Azevedo Gondim wrote the statutes, and in the first session of the general assembly, Padilha was hailed as an Associate Benefactor and Honorary President in Perpetuity.

As far as agriculture, Padilha dug himself into a hole, waiting for equipment catalogs that never arrived. He started running away from me. If he happened to see me, he'd hunch over, pretend to be distracted, pull his hat down. When the first note came due, he got sick. I went to visit and found him hiding in the dining room, playing backgammon with João Nogueira. Seeing me, he got so upset that his fingers—skinny and burnt, with bitten-down nails—trembled as he shook the dice.

From that point on, he was a man possessed. They told me he'd greased his shins to São Bernardo. "What would he be doing there?"

The final note came due one winter day. It was raining hard as God-help-us. Early that morning, I had Casimiro Lopes saddle my horse. I donned my overcoat and set out—six miles in four hours, the road an endless morass. I saw the chimneys of Mendonça's sugar mill and the strip of land always in dispute between him and old Salustiano Padilha. Now Bom-Sucesso's fences were eating into São Bernardo.

I rode up to the manor house, which looked even older and more decrepit in the pouring rain. The spiderweeds hadn't been trimmed. I dismounted and went in, stamping my feet hard, my spurs jingling. Luís Padilha was sleeping in a grimy hammock in the main room, oblivious to the rain lashing the windows and leaks flooding the floor. I shook the hammock's knot. The ex-director of the *Viçosa Mail* got up, dazed. "You? Out here? How's it going?"

"All right. Much appreciated."

I sat down on a bench and presented him with the notes. Padilha looked away with a quiver of distaste. "I've thought about this business, thought a lot. I've lost sleep over it. Yesterday first thing, I wanted to come by and work it out. But I couldn't. Rain like this—"

"Forget the rain."

"I've got serious problems. I wanted to propose an extension, with accumulated interest. I've got no recourse."

"What about the mill, the plows?"

Luís Padilha answered vaguely. "One winter like this screws everything up. I've got no recourse, but the deal is guaranteed. The extension—"

"Not worth it. Let's settle up."

"Settle up now? Didn't I just tell you I can't? Unless you'll take the printing press."

"The printing press? Are you thick?"

"It's what I have. You've got to make do with what you have. I'm not denying I owe you, but how am I supposed to pay like this, with a knife in my chest? If I turned myself upside down today, a nickel wouldn't fall out of my pocket. I'm tapped out."

"Bad form, Padilha. You know perfectly well the notes are due."

"But I don't have the money! Am I supposed to steal? I can't. It's over."

"What's over, you loafer? This is just the beginning. I'm taking everything, you dog. I'm leaving you in your long johns."

The Honorary President in Perpetuity of the Literary and Recreational Guild was startled. "Be patient, Sr. Paulo. All this shouting won't resolve anything. I'll pay. Wait a few days. Debt's only tough for the debtor."

"I'm not waiting a single hour. I'm talking seriously, and you're talking rot. Some nerve. You want to resolve this amicably? Name a price for the property."

Luís Padilha's mouth dropped open and his tiny eyes popped. For him, São Bernardo's sole value was sentimental: it's where he came to hide his bitterness and brokenness, kill small birds, take a dip in the creek, and sleep. He slept a lot because he dreaded coming across Mendonça.

"Name a price."

"Just between us," the lowlife murmured, "I always wanted to keep the ranch."

"For what? São Bernardo's a piece of trash. I'm speaking as a friend. Yessir, as a friend. I have no intention of seeing a pal with a noose around his neck. These lawyers are hungry as wolves, and if I get Nogueira to flick the lighter, you'll be toting your nuts on your back. Not worth it, Padilha. Name a price."

We argued over the transaction until sunset. To start, Luís Padilha asked eighty contos.

"You're insane! Your father would have given it to Fidélis for fifty. And that would have been high. Today, with the mill fallen down, the gates trampled by the neighbors' cattle, the houses in ruins, Mendonça's about to put his claws through whatever shreds..."

I was winded. I took a breath and offered thirty contos. He went down to seventy and changed the subject. When we got back to bargaining, I came up to thirty-two. Padilha chopped it to sixty-five and swore to God in heaven that that was the final word. I likewise declared I wouldn't give up another cent, not worth it. But I tossed out thirty-four. Padilha, for solidarity's sake, agreed to sixty. We debated for two hours, repeating the same charades to no result.

I preached on my journeys in the backlands and followed by insisting indifferently on thirty-four contos, which scored a shift to fifty-five. I showed generosity: thirty-five. Padilha held fast at fifty-five, so I insulted him, declaring that old Salustiano had thrown away the money spent on his schooling. I threatened him with my hands. He backed down to fifty. I advanced to forty and claimed I was robbing myself. At this point, each of us dug in our heels, pulling for his own side. To bolster mine, I invoked Mendonça, swallower of land; the justice officials; the property appraisal; the expenses. The lowlife, terrified, came down to forty-eight. I regretted that I had ventured forty: not worth it, robbery. Padilha slid down to forty-five. I tied myself to forty, then chewed through the rope: "Lower. I'm flat broke."

Minus what he owed me, the rest could be divided into promissory notes. Padilha went crazy: he cried, delivered himself to God, took back what he'd done. Let the lawyer come, let the judge come, let the police come, let the devil come. Let them take it all. Screw the agreement! Screw the law!

"What do I care about the law? Screw it!"

He had means. He didn't exactly have his head on backward. He had means. He'd go to the press gallery, claim his rights, protest this pillaging.

I acted like I sympathized and promised to pay in cash and with a house I had in town, worth ten contos. Padilha set seven contos for the house and forty-three for São Bernardo. I yanked him down two more contos: forty-two for the property and eight for the house. We disputed another half-hour and sealed the deal.

To guard against regrets, I gave Padilha a lift to the city and kept an eye on him overnight. Early the next day, he put his tail in the mousetrap and signed the deed. I deducted the debt, the interest, and the price of the house and handed over seven contos, five hundred and fifty milreis. I felt no remorse.

5

"SIR, YOU did wrong to acquire that property without consulting me," Mendonça shouted from the other side of the fence.

"Why? The former owner wasn't of age?"

"No doubts about that," Mendonça replied, sticking out his white whiskers and his hooked nose. "But you should have informed yourself before you bought into this dispute."

"I'm not looking to argue. I think we understand each other."

"Depends on you, sir. The present boundaries are provisional—did you know that? Best to get that clear. Each keeps to what's his. It's not worth fixing the fence. I'm taking it down so we can figure out where it goes."

I suggested to old Mendonça that he'd already shrunk São Bernardo plenty. "Show me the papers," I said. If we couldn't agree, we'd better bring in a lawyer and a surveyor.

"That's great! Get in good with the officials and you've got me in your pocket. But I'm not taking it. The fence is coming down."

I quickly counted his mestizos and counted mine. No, I said, the fence was not coming down. Polite explanations—sure. Shouts—no.

Then, almost regretful, I relented. It didn't suit me, fighting this crotchety old man. I just didn't want to roll over and show my belly on the first meeting.

Casimiro Lopes stepped forward. I touched his shoulder and he fell back. Mendonça understood the situation. He started treating me with excessive courtesy. I paid him in the same currency and, as he needed some of the cedars over by Bom-Sucesso, I offered them to him. He refused and proposed trading them for some zebu heifers. I declared that I had no intention of creating an Indian herd and spoke enthusiastically about the Limousin and the Schwitz. Mendonça dismissed the finer breeds: they eat so much and can't bear the ticks; it was fattening calves for the butcher.

I insisted on offering him the wood. He started shaking. Our conversation was dry, our speech quick, our smiles cold. The mestizos were suspicious. My heart was thumping as I predicted the consequences of all this deceit. Mendonça scratched his beard.

"As for the boundaries, I think we can resolve that later, calmly."

"Absolutely," Mendonça agreed.

We bid each other goodbye. I continued stretching the wire mesh and replacing the old clamps with new ones. Mendonça, in the distance, kept turning back, smiling, and nailing me with his red eyes.

In the afternoon, when I returned to the house, Casimiro Lopes accompanied me, scowling. When I didn't say anything, he coughed and came to a stop. I leaned on a lemon tree and drove away the terrible ideas chasing me.

"Tomorrow, have four men come and fill in that marsh. And clean out this stream here so the water doesn't flood the plain."

"Is that all?"

I thought how, instead of filling in the marsh, it would have been better to bring Mestre Caetano to work in the quarry. But I didn't contradict myself—doesn't look good for a boss.

"Is that all?" Casimiro Lopes asked again. I caught the thought sliding through his tangled hair, narrow forehead, wide red cheeks, and thick lips. Maybe he was right. I should move cautiously, avoid the scrub, be careful which paths I took. And this house full of holes, with its walls falling down...

I decided to bring in Mestre Caetano and the quarrymen. Damn! I shook my head to clear out a sketchy plan.

"That's all for now."

6

THE SECOND year brought horrendous problems. I planted castor beans and cotton, but the harvest was bad, prices low. Those were dreary months—living hand to mouth, risking my neck, scraping the bottom of the barrel. I worked like the damned, barely sleeping, getting up at four in the morning, spending days on end in sun and rain with a machete, pistol, and bandolier, nothing but a piece of dried cod with a scoop of manioc as a meal on breaks. At night, in my hammock, I spelled out job particulars to Casimiro Lopes. He squatted on a mat and, in spite of his fatigue, listened closely. Sometimes, Shark barked outside and we pricked up our ears.

One time, we thought we heard footsteps near the house. I peeked through a crack in the wall. In the vast darkness, I made out a figure. The footfalls continued. The dog yelped and growled.

"Always something!" Casimiro Lopes murmured.

The following day, I visited Mendonça. He greeted me nervously. We talked about everything, but especially about voting. I paid compliments to his daughters, a couple of single girls, and lamented the death of his wife—an excellent person, caring, loved to look after people, yessir. Mendonça, startled, asked how I knew Dona Alexandrina.

"A long time ago. I was one of old Salustiano's tenant workers. Field hand: I dragged a hoe."

The girls found this gauche, but the father appreciated my honesty, revealing my roots so freely. Then he complained about the neighbors (none of them would have anything to do with him).

"There are some pains in the neck around here who started much like you, sir, and who brag about their status. There's no dishonor in work. If you're born dirt poor, why deny it?" He tried to shame me. "Field hand, huh? Don't let it bother you. Fidélis is highly regarded now, head of a mill. But he used to steal chickens."

I watched him cut down another local, not looking half as agitated as when I'd turned up. All he wanted to talk about was his neighbors' faults, as if he'd forgotten the rest of the world, but maybe it was a trick. I buttered him up, chatting about the elections. It's possible he wasn't fooled, though, playing with me the way I was playing with him. If that's how it was, he put on a good show, but I ultimately convinced myself that he didn't suspect me. I was the one putting on a good show in that case, making him believe I was there to talk politics. If he thought that, he was crazy. Probably didn't, though. Unless he thought it after he was fooled into thinking I was being sincere. That's what happened to me: repeating the same words, the same gestures, listening to the same stories, I ended up liking Bom-Sucesso's owner.

Instinctively, though, I continued watching him. He roused himself. Yawning, showing his pointy yellow canines, he slapped a mosquito.

A mosquito moving like a bullet! He'd slept terribly last night.

I replied that I'd slept like a log. The bogs at São Bernardo were filled in. There wasn't a single mosquito left on my land.

I regretted speaking so hastily. Mendonça gave me a sideways look. I assume he wasn't pleased. He returned to talking about his sleepless night, and I repeated that I had slept. He was insecure, his face twitching. He understood it was a lie, of course.

Each of us lied baldly. I foisted another speech on them about my life as a worker. Mediocre result: the girls nodded off and Mendonça frowned.

A shifty-looking mestizo came into the room. Mendonça furrowed his brow. I wanted to leave but was afraid the moment wasn't right. So I stayed in my seat, hoping to change the disagreeable impression I'd made. The girls apparently thought I was a bore. "If the coming winter's like this one," I said, "it's all going to rack and ruin: everything will turn to mud and not a single cassava will take root."

"So true," Mendonça replied, visibly annoyed with the mestizo, who looked at me calmly without raising his head.

"Anyway, bye for now," I exclaimed suddenly. "The election's on Sunday, huh? Got it. I'll slaughter a ...'"—I was going to say an ox, but I thought better of it; everyone knew I only brought in a half-dozen voters—"a sheep. A sheep's plenty, no? Sounds good. Until Sunday."

And I left, dissatisfied. I'm guessing that's more or less what happened. I don't remember exactly.

I crossed the courtyard and took the shortcut to São Bernardo. For shame! Seizing other people's land and not doing anything about such nasty, swampy footpaths full of chameleons, brushwood whacking the face of anyone passing through!

I crossed the trouble zone. The fence was still standing where I'd found it the year before. Mendonça was struggling to advance but was blocked; I was trying, unsuccessfully, to secure the old boundaries. This was the only serious disagreement: some punk from São Bernardo did wrong by Mendonça's sugar supervisor's daughter. Mendonça, in return, took pliers to the wire mesh. But I'd mended the fence and arranged a marriage between the punk and the little mulatta.

I glanced over the cotton fields and set out for the wall of the dam. Not many workers.

I climbed the hill. I'd finished the foundations of this house, our house, and the walls were coming up. All of a sudden, there was a bang. I winced. It was in the quarry, which Mestre Caetano was slowly excavating with two quarrymen. Another bang, a bad one, and a tiny stone came flying.

When would these layabouts be finished? Sadly, I didn't have the resources to get after them properly. Even with so few hands, sometimes on a Friday I didn't know where to find the money to pay Saturday's wages.

I asked the mason some questions. One single mason. The walls were a meter high. It would be cheaper if I could hire more laborers. The rock wall for the weir wasn't going ahead— it was going backward. After six months of work, the quarry, where a few tiny figures moved around, looked untouched.

An oxcart passed below me; another oxcart arrived, carrying bricks.

Where could old Margarida have wandered off to? It would be good to find the old lady and bring her to São Bernardo. She had to be closing in on a century now, poor thing.

I hung around until the workers had washed the shovels and put away their tools. I was alone. The farm laborers were scattering and the ones from the dam too.

A few last bangs from the quarry. I thought about Men-

donça. Cur. On this side of the fence, the cotton was green-
ing and castor beans were coming up in the burnt clearings.
On the other side, straw and thorns. How many yards of
land that lowlife had stolen! Good thing we were at peace.
Supposedly. In any case, I needed to move fast.

I went down the hill and home for lunch. While I ate, I
talked in a low voice to Casimiro Lopes, handling him with
kid gloves at first, then outlining a plan. Casimiro Lopes
dropped the kid gloves and signed on to the plan.

That business begun, I closed the doors and wrote to some
banks in the capital as well as to the state governor. I asked
the banks for loans; I told the governor about the many
industrial facilities nearby and asked for a tax break on
machinery I wanted to import. Truth was, the loans weren't
likely and I couldn't imagine how to pay for the machinery,
but I'd gotten used to thinking of them as practically bought.

Following this, I checked with the Agricultural Institute
of Satuba about the possible acquisition of a Limousin bull
calf.

As I finished, I heard footsteps outside the house. I got
up and looked through the crack. A fellow was snapping his
fingers, trying to fool Shark. The closer I looked, the more
he resembled the shifty customer who'd come into Mendonça's living room. I left my post, telling Casimiro Lopes
to take my place. As I lay down, my mind went to Mestre
Caetano and the quarry. Mallets, chisels, steel borers, gun-
powder, fuses.

"Folks from over there," Casimiro Lopes whispered, rock-
ing the knot of the hammock.

"Definitely."

The next day, Saturday, I killed a sheep for the voters.
Sunday afternoon, returning from the election, Mendonça

got shot in his littlest rib and kicked the bucket, right on the street, close to Bom-Sucesso. There's a cross there today with an arm missing.

At the time of the crime, I was in the city, talking with the vicar about the church I was planning to put up on São Bernardo. In the future, if business went well.

"How horrible!" exclaimed Padre Silvestre when the news arrived. "Did he have enemies?"

"Enemies? You bet! Like ticks. But moving on, Padre Silvestre. How much is a bell?"

7

AROUND this time I met an old fellow called Ribeiro, going nowhere fast at Brito's *Gazeta* in Maceió: tall, stooped,
skinny, jaundiced, side-whiskered. He obviously wasn't getting enough to eat. I felt for him and, since I needed a bookkeeper, brought him to São Bernardo. I paid him some
attention and listened to his story, which I will now reproduce
here, putting the verbs in the third person but using language
otherwise meant to sound like his.

Sr. Ribeiro was seventy years old and unhappy, but once
he had been young and happy. In the village where he lived,
men would take off their hats when they saw him and women
would lower their heads and say, "Blessed be Our Lord Jesus
Christ, major."

When anyone received letters, they'd ask him to interpret
them. Sr. Ribeiro would read the letters and learn their secrets. He was respected, a major.

When two neighbors fought over land, Sr. Ribeiro sum-
moned them, studied the case, determined the boundaries,
and requested all disputants to stick to them.

Everyone believed in the major's wisdom. In point of fact,
Sr. Ribeiro was no ignoramus: he'd memorize laws, old ones,
reread journals, old ones, and, by the light of an oil lamp,
wear his eyes out over books full of mysterious, hard-to-
pronounce words. When he figured out one of those strange

29

words, he would explain it to the village, expanding their vocabulary.

The others? They were ignorant. Sometimes one of these ignorant creatures turned up dead, clubbed or knifed. Sr. Ribeiro, who was a just man, would find the killer, tie him up, and lock him in the city jail. The major protected the family of the deceased.

Other times some girl would start by sobbing and end up confessing she was with child. Sr. Ribeiro would expose the seducer and call the priest. The wedding would take place in the village chapel. When the child was born, Sr. Ribeiro was named godfather.

The major's decisions were beyond appeal. Each decision was a nail.

There were no soldiers in this place, no judge. And since the vicar lived far away, Sr. Ribeiro's wife said the rosary and recounted the lives of the saints for the children. Maybe not all of the stories were true, but children back then weren't as worried about the truth.

Sr. Ribeiro had a small family and a large house. The house was always full. His cotton fields were also large. The people worked hard at harvesttime. Blacks didn't know they were black, and whites didn't know they were white.

Without question, Sr. Ribeiro drew respect. If there was a ruckus in the market, he'd raise a hand, shouting, "Anyone on my side, come with me!" And the market would shut down, the ruckus over. Everyone followed the major because everyone was on his side.

On the nights of the São João festival, an enormous bonfire lit up his house. There were bonfires in front of the other houses, but his bonfire was piled high with firewood. Young girls and boys circled it, arm in arm. They roasted green corn on the embers and fired shots on the blunderbuss, making a terrific racket. The major owned a blunderbuss, but only cleaned the rust off for São João festivities.

Now, these things happened long ago.

Everything changed. People were born, people died, the major's godchildren grew up and left by train to join the military.

The village became a town, the town became a city, with an elected official, a justice of the peace, a public prosecutor, and a police chief.

Machines arrived and the major's cotton mill ground to a halt.

A vicar arrived who closed the chapel and constructed a fine church. The stories of the saints died in the children's memories.

A doctor arrived. He didn't believe in the saints. Sr. Ribeiro's wife grew sad and thin, and withered away.

A lawyer opened a consultancy, the major's wisdom retreated, and disputes arose in the courts.

Sure enough, the city developed quickly. Men put on ties and new professions. Oxcarts no longer creaked in the narrow streets. Automobiles, gasoline, electricity, and cinema. Taxes.

Young girls and boys no longer circled the São João bonfires arm in arm. They danced the tango or the *frevo*.

One day, Sr. Ribeiro realized he was living in a house that was much too big. He sold it for a small one. By this time, people did what they wanted; his authority as good as gone.

He had a son who played soccer and a daughter who wore ribbons, lots of ribbons. The place was too backward, they thought, and fled. Sr. Ribeiro hid away, full of shame. He mourned for a week, then sold off his odds and ends to go in search of his children. He never found them: they'd wandered off—she to the factories, he to the army.

Sr. Ribeiro settled in the capital. He got to know the indigents' hospital, slept on park benches, sold lottery tickets for the state and then for the mob, a hustler in the rattraps. At the tail end of ten years, he was the *Gazeta*'s manager and bookkeeper, with a salary of a hundred and fifty milreis, and was begging friends for money.

When the old fellow finished dribbling out his tale, I exclaimed, "It's like you left your legs under a car back there, Sr. Ribeiro. Couldn't you move any faster? What the hell."

8

THE SHIFTY-looking mestizo I'd met that day at Mendonça's also came to a bad end. A cleanup. These people
almost never die right. Some are taken out by snakes, others
by cachaça; some kill each other.

I lost one in the quarry. The chisel jumped out from
under a stone, hit him in the chest, and he bought the farm.
He left a widow and tiny orphans. They all vanished: one of
the kids fell in the fire, roundworms ate the second, the last
had a heart condition, and the wife hanged herself.

To reduce mortality and increase productivity, I prohib-
ited cane liquor.

I finished constructing my new house. No need to describe
it. The main parts have appeared or will soon; the rest is ex-
pendable, interesting to architects, maybe, but they probably
won't read this. Everything was cozy and attractive. I stopped
sleeping in a hammock, of course. I bought furniture and
other stuff I was too shy to use. There are things I still haven't
used, even today, because I don't know what they're for.

Here we jump five years. In five years, the world turns
many times.

Given all the hardships I've described, I doubt anyone
could think that I was tripping along, safe and secure, trotting down a straight and narrow path without pauses or
detours. No sir, I didn't trip and I didn't trot. There were

low times, when I wanted to back out, obstacles to get around, twists and turns. Do you think I did wrong? Truth is, I'll never know which of my actions were good or bad. I did good things that worked against me and bad things that made me money. Since I always kept my goal in sight—owning São Bernardo—anything that got me there was right as far as I was concerned.

I accomplished more than I'd hoped, by God's grace. I got wrinkles, anyone can see that, but the credit I was initially denied now came my way with lowered interest rates. Business doubled, automatically. Automatically. Tough? Not at all! Once things are on track, they roll along beautifully. If they don't, sit back and wait. But if luck's on your side, say what you want, you can do stupid things that pay off. I've seen folks working way too hard for nothing. And I know lazy people who can smell the first hint of opportunity. They unscrew their lids, open wide, and swallow it all.

I'm not lazy. I was happy with my earliest efforts and made fortune shine on whatever came after.

After Mendonça's death, I took down the fence, of course, and put it up beyond where it was in Salustiano Padilha's time. There were objections.

"My good ladies, Sr. Mendonça pushed the envelope while he was alive. But this is how things are now. If you don't like it, be patient. Take it to court."

But justice is expensive, so they didn't take it to court. With the way cleared, I also invaded Fidélis's land—he's paralyzed in one arm—and the Gamas'. They were merry-making in Recife, studying law. I respected Sr. Magalhães's mill—he's a judge.

Tiny violations go unseen. The more serious disputes were won in court, thanks to João Nogueira's skullduggery.

I carried out some risky transactions, got myself in debt, importing machinery and paying no heed to anyone who griped about my wanting to take over the world. I started orchards and raised poultry. To get the goods to market, I started paving a road. Azevedo Gondim wrote a couple of articles about it, called me a patriot, making reference to Ford and Delmiro Gouveia. Costa Brito also published a note in the *Gazeta*, singing my praises and the praises of the local elected official. He got one hundred milreis out of me for that.

All this advertising notwithstanding, difficulties arose. As long as I was poking around at São Bernardo, everything went well, but when I dug into four or five other properties, I tripped on a hornet's nest. Lost two mestizos and took a shot in an ambush. Flesh wound: so I've got a scar on my shoulder. Exasperated, I paid another hundred milreis to Costa Brito and sent for João Nogueira and Gondim: "Distract that herd of asses. Look, I'm doing a public service and I don't collect taxes. It's a crying shame. The county should be supporting me. Talk to the mayor, Sr. Nogueira. See if he can get me a couple barrels of cement for cattle guards."

I didn't get the cement, but I still built the cattle guards. My ambitious plans and unusual methods meant all the small-minded people thought I was crazy and left me to myself.

Around this time, we had a visit from the state governor. It had been three years since the dam was completed—asinine, according to Fidélis. Why have a dam where there's a stream that never runs dry?

It really didn't appear to do much, but a little ways out there was a sluice: the water ran the cotton gin and the sawmill.

The governor liked the orchard, the Orpington hens, the cotton, and the castor beans. He thought Limousin bulls sounded about right, requested photographs, and asked where the school would go. I told him it wasn't going anywhere.

At lunch, we had champagne. Sr. Magalhães proclaimed a toast. His Excellency turned the talk toward a school. I wanted to interrupt, but restrained myself. A school! What's it to me if people can read or not? "These government men have got a screw loose. Try sending educated people out to pick castor beans. See what kind of harvest you get."

Getting up from the table, Padilha, glassy-eyed, asked me in a low voice for fifty milreis.

"Not a cent."

I showed our illustrious guest the sawmill, the cotton gin, and the stable. I described the press, the generator, the saws, and the acaricide bath. Suddenly, I wondered if the school might make the governor shine some benevolence on certain favors I hoped for.

"But of course, sir. Next time Your Excellency comes, everyone will be cracking open schoolbooks."

Later on, taking in a view of the countryside from the church foundation, I pulled the lawyer aside. "Look, Sr. Nogueira, send Padilha over here tomorrow. I need to talk with him, but the wretch can barely stand. Don't forget, you hear? Tomorrow, after he's slept off his drunk."

His Excellency bid us goodbye. The date was stamped forever in memory. The cars rolled off down the road. Looking at the cloud of dust they raised, I rubbed my hands.

"Luck of the devil! This visit is going to do me a world of good. It's cash in the bank—wonder how much."

Truth is, well setup though I looked, I'd been surprised

by some creditors. Things were going well, no doubt—better liquid assets than liabilities—but if those miscreants wanted to, they could geld me. Now those fears ebbed. The school was money in the bank. The church foundation too.

I continued rubbing my hands. Luck of the devil! I decided to offer protection to the Mendonça girls. My fortunes rose after their father's death. Back then, a few yards of good soil meant a lot to me, the tiniest bit of good soil.

I felt sorry for the Mendonças. I'd send someone the next day to clean up the Bom-Sucesso cotton fields. The plants were stunted, overgrown with brush. They'd come way down in the world, those Mendonça girls. Their father was a swindler, but was that the poor things' fault? I resolved to keep an eye out to make sure no unscrupulous neighbors tried to appropriate anything. Women practically never defend themselves. Well, if any of those villains tried to do them wrong, they'd have me to deal with.

9

THE NEXT day, when we got back from the fields, I found João Nogueira, Padilha, and Azevedo Gondim on my veranda, raving on about some curves. They elevated the level of the conversation.

"A cultured woman," João Nogueira affirmed. "Educated."

"And earnest," added Azevedo Gondim.

"Truly," Padilha murmured, scraping his nails out with a match. He couldn't think of any quality that would compare with her curves.

João Nogueira remembered that he was a man of responsibilities. A lawyer, more than forty years old, respectably bald. Once in a while, he'd go on a spree, but with clients he was all business. I'd given him four contos, eight hundred a year for legal help to improve São Bernardo, so in front of me he displayed good sense and a kind of pedantry.

I called him "sir." I couldn't treat him familiarly. I considered myself superior to him, except with less learning and less cunning. It seemed to me his talents deserved a certain scorn, but they had their uses. There was a goodly amount of respect between us.

"We kept our man Padilha company," said Nogueira. "Came on foot, since the afternoon was cool enough to make for a pleasant walk. I'm here to consult with you."

Silently, I invited them in, glancing over at a window

where Sr. Ribeiro's white whiskers and spectacles showed above the account books. We went into the study. It was the first of the month. I opened the cashbox and handed over two bills of two hundred each to the lawyer. Sr. Ribeiro detailed a shaky entry in the blotter and discreetly withdrew. Sitting, João Nogueira handed over the receipt, took some papers out of his briefcase, and gave me an account of various lawsuits. From the first, I could tell the four hundred milreis were well spent; the lawsuits were all coming along nicely. But the notary didn't inspire my trust. Nor did the justice of the peace. I needed to fix their fences.

"Go ahead. Make promises, Sr. Nogueira. Don't advance a cent—promise. Pay in the end if they're honest."

He filled me in on some uninteresting details, and I gave some instructions to Ribeiro. We went back to the porch, where Luís Padilha and Azevedo Gondim had started raving about those curves again.

"Whose curves are these?"

"Madalena's," responded Gondim.

"Who?"

"A teacher. You don't know her? Pretty."

João Nogueira cut him off. "Educated."

"Pretty," Gondim said once more. "A little blond, about thirty."

"How old?" asked João Nogueira.

"About thirty, give or take."

"Twenty, if that."

"You never saw her close up." Gondim broke in. "If you had, you wouldn't be babbling that way."

"How do you get that? I've seen her close up plenty of times, at Magalhães's house, at Marcela's birthday party. She's twenty."

"It's because you saw her at night. Things look different in the morning. She's thirty."

Padilha, gazing morosely on the heifers grazing in the molasses grass along the creek and the ducks swimming behind the dam, sighed and suggested twenty-five. "That's how old she is. Twenty-five."

I stretched my arms, tired after a long day in the sun, fighting with workers. "Fine, Padilha, twenty-five and we'll call it even. Have you all had supper or not? You can take the car back later. Padilha, I need to talk with you."

Yesterday evening, I'd sent Luís Padilha a message. He was curious, rattling it around in his gourd.

"Listen. I think I want to open a school."

"Magnificent!" exclaimed Azevedo Gondim with a smile that flattened his nose even more. "You took my advice, huh? There's nothing like education."

The lawyer ran his fingertips across his forehead and predicted, offhandedly, that the school would be extremely useful.

"Who knows?" I shrugged my shoulders. "I don't believe it—obviously, since I'm hiring Padilha. Sure we could set up a good rural school, give a reasonable education in agriculture and cattle-raising. But where are we going to find experts? And so much money! For now it'll just be a smattering of reading, writing, and arithmetic. Do you think you're up to looking after this, Padilha?"

Luís Padilha inquired about the pay, saying he had a lot of work at the moment.

Slowly, the electric lights grew brighter. Lights also came on in the tenant workers' houses. As if those wretches crowded down there at the bottom of Bom-Sucesso's fences had ever even thought of electric lights. Light till midnight. Comfort! And I was planning to install telephones.

Casimiro Lopes limped closer.

"Let's go have supper. I asked you to come over, Padilha, because I thought you needed work. But if you're too busy, that's that. Let's go eat."

Over supper, Azevedo Gondim said why he had come: he'd discovered the whereabouts of old Margarida.

"What are you saying, Gondim? And you were keeping mum?"

Azevedo Gondim filled his glass. "She lives in Jacaré dos Homens."

"Where is that?"

"In Pão de Açucar. I got a letter today. Birthmarks, age, skin color, everything lines up. She lives with a family of cheesemakers. I've already pulled the advertisement from the *Cruzeiro*."

"Right. Do you all know anyone in Pão de Açucar? Sr. Ribeiro, you know anyone in Pão de Açucar?"

They didn't.

"Look, Gondim, since you're already on the job, ask the vicar who wrote to Padre Soares about bringing her. I'm thinking I'll go with you all. I'm going to speak with Padre Silvestre. Make sure to transport the woman carefully so she's not wrecked by the trip. And when she gets here, you can order your knickknacks, Gondim. What did you call them?"

"Stereotypes. Stereotypes and plates."

"Exactly. You can send for your stereotypes and plates, once we have the old lady."

"I've been thinking about the school," murmured Padilha.

"Me too. You took the words right out of my mouth," João Nogueira interrupted. "Offer it to Madalena, Sr. Paulo Honório. An excellent acquisition, an educated woman."

"She would spruce up the place, Sr. Paulo!" shouted Azevedo Gondim.

"Ridiculous. Am I trinket-shopping?"

Padilha, a little perturbed, snorted, clutching his bone. "I never said I wouldn't accept. I just said I have a lot of work. But I also asked what the salary is."

Busy pulling a wing off the chicken, I didn't respond.

"I asked what the salary is," Padilha repeated timidly.

Poor sod! So tiny, so annoying, like a bedbug.

"Depends. I don't know what you're worth. Maybe a hundred milreis a month. Let's make it a hundred and fifty for a trial period. Lodging, food, great conversation, a hundred and fifty milreis a month and eight hours of work a day. Sound good? But be warned: work is work, and there's no drinking around here. Drinking is for guests only."

"Perfect." Padilha chewed, abashed. "I'll consider it. As for drinking, you don't even need to say anything, since I don't drink. Maybe at mealtimes, but not always, just a glass now and again if my friends insist. I'll give some thought to the offer."

We finished supper in silence. Maria das Dores brought coffee and cleared the plates. I opened the cigar box and lit my pipe. We moved to the living room.

Sr. Ribeiro unfolded the *Gazeta*. I instinctively hid myself in a corner, away from the open doors. There was one window I couldn't avoid. I wanted to close it, but then I relaxed: Casimiro Lopes, who guarded the house, went to sit on one of the unfinished church walls, the rifle snugged between his legs, and stayed there, unmoving, sniffing the air.

"So our Padilha will return to São Bernardo," said João Nogueira.

"And finish the book," Azevedo Gondim added. "With your life all organized, you'll write like heck, Padilha."

"As if!" He was ashamed of having written stories published in the *Cruzeiro* pseudonymously. Whenever anyone mentioned them, he thought they were scoffing and got flustered. He drew himself up, casting a bitter glance over the chairs, floor, lamps. "The salary is so low it won't even cover books. But I'll come. I'll come for the cause of education. And because I may be headed for a teaching career."

Sr. Ribeiro turned the newspaper pages, moving his lips, gesticulating at times. Offensive, the *Gazeta*—Brito's requests for money were getting unbearable.

Tired after covering more than five miles on foot, Azevedo Gondim yawned and stretched. "So Pereira's people were defeated, huh?"

Municipal election.

"Not interested. Ghost candidates!"

I'm okay with truly taking sides: I used to send my voters to the ballot boxes and get the party's thanks in exchange. But minor local trickery? No. If Pereira had slipped on a banana skin, so much the worse for him: he'd drop out and someone new would come along and be added to the slate.

"Good thing," muttered Padilha, who had never forgiven Pereira for being skeptical of his farming plans. "That man's a jackass."

"How unfair!" cried João Nogueira, smiling. "Pereira has always been a man of tact."

Everyone prated on about his wisdom, but here's Padilha calling him a jackass.

"My man," Azevedo Gondim ventured, stroking his beard,

"it's not just Padilha. Me too. And you. In a moment like this, it's banging your head against a wall. If we had a cabal elected at the federal level, it might be worth it. But when the government doesn't care about votes and wants to put Padre Silvestre in city hall? Padilha has a point."

"Come on!" I cut him off. "Gondim, you supported the vicar's candidacy in the newspaper, didn't you?"

"Sure, I supported it. I supported it out of political solidarity. But privately, I disagreed. Nogueira was there. He'll vouch for me. And as for saying it was garbage, it was."

I knew that Padre Silvestre had spoken of cutting the monthly grant of one hundred and fifty milreis that the city gave the *Cruzeiro*. It was a knife held to Gondim's throat. Full of rage, he defended the vicar, extolling his virtues and leaving aside the rest of the agenda.

"What a disaster. A good man. So what. He's naive, easily swayed by rumor—the intelligence of a newly hatched turkey, slow as a snail."

"Priests!" exclaimed Luís Padilha with scorn. He was an atheist and a quick-change artist. After I had relieved him of the ranch, he'd gotten bloodthirsty ideas and preached, under his breath, the extermination of the bourgeois. "Cur!" He gnawed furiously at his nails.

Sr. Ribeiro, his eyes keen, made disapproving gestures, commenting on Brito's bad writing.

"What I don't understand, what I find strange, is why the vicar tumbled. He was almost elected, recognized, sworn in, and suddenly—pow!—on the floor. What happened?"

"Padre Silvestre is a revolutionary," explained João Nogueira. "He plans to save the country by violent means."

I shuddered. Casimiro Lopes held a lighter to his cigarette.

The moon shone very white. A slice of the distant woods appeared, making the pau d'arcos' yellow flowers stand out.

I got up and signaled João Nogueira. We approached the window.

"Say, Sr. Nogueira, tell me one thing," I said quietly. "Is this story about Pereira's downfall a sure thing?"

João Nogueira accepted a cigar and declared that there was no doubt whatsoever. "The governor is reasonable and proposed a compromise, putting the priest on the council. Pereira gambled on the priest and lost."

"All right, Sr. Nogueira," I murmured, lowering my voice even more. "Be on the lookout for a suitable occasion to liquidate my dealings with Pereira. I've been fence-sitting, watching the tide, because he was boss. But if he's down in the muck, that's all done. He's on the hook for an account so old it's turning gray. I'll hand it over to you. See if you can get me a mortgage."

"Excellent," agreed João Nogueira, getting enthusiastic. "Absolutely excellent! Authorize the power of attorney. You'll be doing the party a great service, sir. Put the squeeze on Pereira, Sr. Paulo Honório."

10

AROUND here, workers see saints' days as occasions to take trips, get sick, and otherwise play hooky. Sunday's a loss and Saturday's already gone to the market—a week only has five days, and the church cuts them down that much more. The result? Pay shrinks and everybody goes about with rumbling stomachs.

On one of these fake holidays, when I couldn't find anyone to pull the water hyacinths out of the dam and clear out some scrub, I distracted myself by listening to Padilha and Casimiro Lopes talking about jaguars.

They don't understand each other. Padilha, a skinny bourgeois, talks nonstop and reveres violent actions; Casimiro Lopes is lame, with a meager vocabulary. He thinks the schoolmaster is a superior being because he works with books. When he wants to show how he feels, he widens his eyes and whistles softly. He stammers. In the backcountry, he passed hours in silence—when he was feeling happy, he sang to the bulls. He maybe knows half a dozen words at most. Lately, he'd picked up a few phrases, from eavesdropping on city folk, that he mangled or misused. On this day, hard as he tried, all he'd managed to say was that jaguars are vicious, crafty beasts.

"Spotted! Huge teeth, huge feet, and ... and claws! Horrendous!"

Padilha made him repeat the description, adding details of his own. Casimiro Lopes disagreed but gave in, putting his faith in Padilha's learning. In a matter of minutes, the jaguar had turned into an animal like no one had ever seen.

"Hey, Casimiro, I need you to take a note to the vicar."

I wrote to Padre Silvestre thanking him for his interest in Margarida's difficult journey. She'd arrived a few days ago and was lodged in a little house nestled among banana trees.

I handed the letter over to Casimiro Lopes, got my hat, and went to pay a second visit to the old colored lady. I went down the stairs. Crossing the big wall of the dam, I frightened a cloud of wild ducks and shorebirds. The weir was swollen from the recent rains, with banks of water hyacinth threatening to clog the drain valve. The sluice that ran to the cotton gin and sawmill was overflowing. Sawmill closed, cotton gin closed. Another day lost.

I found Margarida sitting on a mat, scratching at the bricks with charcoal.

"Mother Margarida. How are you today, ma'am?"

She tried to straighten her stiff back, recognizing me by my voice even before casting her white eyes on me.

"I'm here wailing and crying, my son, full of sins."

Sins! Back in the olden days, she was a saint. And now: tiny, huddled, barely moving, barely thinking—what sins could she have? She was nearly blind, so she spoke without lifting her head and gave me the same advice she used to give me when I was a kid. Seized by tenderness, I came closer and sat down next to her on the mat.

"Mother Margarida, I searched for you for a long time. I never forgot. I was overjoyed when I found you. If you want anything, just say so. I'll get anything you need, Mother Margarida, don't be shy."

She looked with amazement at the chairs, the coffee table, the electric lamp, the furniture in the next room.

"What's all this luxury for? Keep your stuff. Maybe it's good for something. I don't sleep in a bed. Waste not, want not."

"No harm in it, Mother Margarida. Be easy. Sleep easy. If you need wood, let me know. Don't let the fire go out. The nights are cold."

"That's what I need, the fire. The fire and a pot."

She went on scratching shapes on the floor. When she leaned forward, a rosary of white and blue beads appeared at her open collar, knocking against her wrinkled breasts.

"And I'd like a pan. They stole the other one."

I remembered the old pan, the centerpiece of the tiny house where we lived. My life revolved around it for years. I washed it, scrubbed the tarnish out with sand and ashes, was sustained by it. Margarida used it almost all her life. Or it used her. Now, decrepit, she couldn't make sweets anymore. Her old utensils were useless.

"All right, Mother Margarida. You'll have a pan just like the other one."

11

ONE DAY, I woke up thinking about marriage—an idea that came to me without a single skirt swishing by. I didn't pay romance much heed, as you may have noted. It always seemed to me that woman was a strange beast, difficult to control.

I had known Marciano's Rosa—very common. I'd also known Germana and others of that ilk. I judged all womankind by them. But what I woke up feeling wasn't an inclination toward any of them: I wanted an heir for São Bernardo.

I tried conjuring a tall, healthy creature, thirty years old, with black hair . . . then ground to a halt. I have no imagination, so these characteristics were all disjointed, never coming together into an actual human form. I thought back on ladies I'd known: Dona Emília Mendonça, one of the Gamas, Azevedo Gondim's sister, and the judge's daughter, Dona Marcela.

At this point, a minor setback arose. One afternoon, I surprised Luís Padilha as he was lecturing Marciano and Casimiro Lopes by the chapel's sidewall (the chapel was finished, minus paint).

"Robbery. It's been categorically proven by philosophers and published in books. Look around: more than five miles of land, houses, woods, a dam, cattle, everything that makes a man. It's not right."

That worn-out mulatto Marciano lapped it up, stretching

and goggling and showing his gappy gums. "You've got a point, Sr. Padilha, sir. I don't understand, I'm a lout, but I'm losing sleep pondering this. We kill ourselves for the sake of others. Isn't that so, Casimiro?"

Casimiro Lopes wrinkled his nose, declaring that things had had owners since the beginning of the world.

"What kind of owner?" Padilha shouted. "Here we are dying, working to make others rich."

I came out of the sacristy and broke it up. "Working on what? What exactly are you working on, you parasitic lazy drudge?"

"Nothing, nothing, Sr. Paulo," Padilha defended himself, trembling. "I was just developing some theories with the guys."

I shot off a barrel of insults at the both of them and told them to pack up and go to hell. "Not on my land." I'd gotten hoarse already. "Scram! Inside these gates, no one pisses except where I say. Take your gibberish and go to hell. Great shape I'm in, with a teacher like this. Easy to see what this ingrate is teaching his students."

But later, shamming, full of lamentation, Padilha swore by all the saints that the school was going great, that it'd break his heart to leave so many children without the fruits of learning. As for his theories, those were just to kill time and make a fool of Casimiro.

"Would I wave a red flag in front of a bull? Do I even seem capable of propagating subversive ideas?"

The next morning, Rosa—weeping, babbling, begging—came with five children (three clinging to her skirts, one in her arms, one in her belly) and cornered me in the orchard. I have no special authority with her, but I put her at ease. "We'll see. Send me that dog Marciano. I'll see you soon."

That night, I met with Marciano and Padilha in the dining room, and bellowed out a long sermon to prove *I* was the one working for *them*. I got muddled halfway, though, and settled for abusing them. "Miscreants. Idiots."

They cowered as I put them down.

"Birdbrains. Taking off in a leaky canoe! Dopes."

I offered them advice. Seeing me soften, Luís Padilha started arguing. I got angry and he convinced himself he was wrong. Marciano retreated into himself, lifting his shoulders as if to pull his head into his body, like a turtle. Padilha gnawed his nails.

"I'll let it go this time. But if I hear tell of you two jumping around like fleas, I'm going to call the police. This isn't Russia, you hear? Now disappear."

They disappeared. I was peeved for a bit, then I quieted down. "Make like nothing happened." Lies. All these idiots sleep too much and say whatever they want. "Marciano, poor sod, he's not really like that. He treats the cattle well, and he's Rosa's husband." As for Padilha, nothing would give me greater pleasure than humiliating him by showing off all the improvements I'd made to the property.

I started again mentally drawing up the woman I referred to at the beginning of this chapter. I saw the Mendonça woman again, the Gama, Gondim's sister (I didn't know what she was called), and Sr. Magalhães's daughter, Dona Marcela. Dona Marcela was a dish. What eyes! On the negative side, she wore too much makeup and lisped. No help for it: no one but God is perfect.

I was wavering on whether to go over to Sr. Magalhães's when Costa Brito came at me with a letter asking for an advance of two hundred milreis.

Costa Brito had turned. The *Gazeta* had always furiously praised the government, but now a contract from the state deputy had flipped the paper over to the opposition. Suddenly, Brito discovered that the public administration was disorganized, in the hands of incompetents. For those of us who voted for the ruling party, but who were neither fish nor fowl, it was all accusations, insults, scorn. On my last trip to the capital, the *Gazeta*'s director cadged another fifty milreis off me in a café where he was indignantly drinking beer—this for a miserable four-line story. "They want write-ups for free. To hell with them! You spend your whole life writing like the damned, lying, to give these boys a leg up. Think of the expense! The price of paper alone! And then, come election time, they kick you in the teeth. Not even a filthy castoff some illiterate mayor could manage. They want compliments. The hell with them."

I didn't need Brito, but I handed over the money in consideration of past favors and because I don't like fighting with members of the press. Later on, I alluded to the crisis and gave him to understand that he couldn't continue to bleed me.

But Brito had the belly of an emu. He disregarded my warning and sent me all kinds of letters, first pleading, then demanding. The one that came in the middle of my wedding plans contained threats.

I sent off a telegram:

USELESS TO INSIST. FED UP.

Pretty to think I was sweating to support a writer. Was I his father?

"Reap what you sow." He can gouge me once in a while, sure—reasonably, in moderation. Threats? No. Blackmail? No.

What the devil would he say against me in the paper? I wasn't a public official. My relations with the party were limited to bringing in voters, handing them the electoral slate, contributing toward the band and fireworks at the governor's receptions. The *Gazeta*'s poison wouldn't affect me. Unless it started messing in my personal affairs. In that case, I'd just have to get a stick and break Brito's ribs.

I stifled these violent thoughts, forcing myself again to conjure up images of Dona Marcela's makeup and lisp. The images arrived, though they slipped away from time to time, with Marciano, Rosa and her kids, Luís Padilha, and Costa Brito popping up in the gaps.

12

THE PEREIRA question was snoozing in city hall, waiting for the district judge to run a pen over the documents, or so João Nogueira told me one afternoon. Connecting Pereira's case with Dona Marcela's endowments, I went down to the city the following day, determined to drop in on Judge Magalhães.

I met him that evening in his living room, which also served as his office, with his daughter and three visitors: João Nogueira; a tall, thin old lady in black; and a younger lady, blond and pretty.

They were sitting quietly in two groups, men separate from women.

Judge Magalhães is very short, with a big nose and a pince-nez and, behind the pince-nez, small bright eyes. He keeps his thin lips pressed together, only unsticking them to talk about himself. Although when he gets onto that subject, he won't stop.

In this moment, however, they were all silent, like I said. Dona Marcela smiled at the young blond woman, who smiled back, showing small white teeth. As I compared the two of them, half of the reason for my visit fell away.

Putting Dona Marcela aside, I attempted, indirectly, to wrest from the judge those words my lawyer needed to hear.

Magalhães ran his hand over his forehead and asked, "Sir, which journals do you subscribe to?"

Agricultural magazines, the party newsletter, the *Cruzeiro,* and the *Gazeta,* I responded. I praised Azevedo Gondim and ran Brito down: "Brash, isn't he?"

Magalhães was evasive. João Nogueira went to a bookcase with two shelves, pulled out a book, sat down again, and started reading.

From the other side of the room came a low murmuring and, occasionally, giggles.

I had to think about something, so I thought about this strange habit of separating males from females. When they come together, it's almost always something to do with sex. Maybe that's why innocent gestures spur malicious gossip. If I greet a lady, she's supposed to recoil, bristling. If she doesn't recoil or bristle, some passerby who has nothing to do with any of it will swear something indecent's going on.

"You haven't put in an appearance at the cinema recently, have you?" the woman in black asked in a loud voice.

"It's been fifteen days, Dona Glória," responded Dona Marcela. "I think it's been fifteen days. Papa, how long has it been since we've gone to the cinema?"

Magalhães calculated. He took a cigar out of his pocket, cut it into two pieces, rolled one into a thin cigarillo, and lit up. "Two weeks."

"That's it exactly, fifteen days."

"No," Magalhães disagreed. "Two weeks. You're mistaken."

"Two weeks aren't fifteen days?" Dona Marcela asked.

"No. Two weeks are fourteen days."

Dona Marcela wasn't convinced. "I've always heard it said that two weeks are fifteen days."

"I've also heard that," Sr. Magalhães acknowledged. "I've heard it many times. But it's wrong. A week has seven days. Isn't seven and seven fourteen? And so? It's fourteen."

João Nogueira threw down his book and said perhaps Dona Marcela was counting the day of the cinema.

"It's possible," Sr. Magalhães conceded. "But not counting that, it's fourteen."

"But counting that, it's fifteen!" shouted Dona Marcela.

"It's better not to count it," Magalhães advised.

Everyone was agitated and the blond girl made a move to get up.

"It's awfully early," murmured Dona Marcela.

The lady in black stayed seated and raised the topic of novels. Dona Marcela had finished one, an adventure story. She tried to see if she could remember the plot, but she got stuck and was uncertain on the characters' names. She began again and got stuck again. "A very tasteful novel, Dona Glória."

"I don't like literature," said Sr. Magalhães. "I flipped through a few books in the old days. But not anymore. I haven't the first clue about all that. I'm only a judge. A judge!"

Dona Marcela had gotten almost positive about the plot of the adventure novel. Dona Glória listened. The blond had bent her head and folded her small hands—beautiful hands, a beautiful head.

"When I judge," announced Sr. Magalhães, "I'm impartial, at a distance from my emotions."

"I said that very thing yesterday to Sr. Nogueira," I interjected.

Sr. Magalhães thanked me. "To work that way it's necessary to have independence. I have independence. What can they do to me? I don't need them."

I had no idea who Sr. Magalhães was talking about. João Nogueira touched him on the shoulder and whispered. He was bringing up the Pereira matter, I realized.

I got up and moved away, so as not to compromise the judge's integrity and to seem halfway polite. At the window, I lit my pipe.

Dona Marcela finished telling the story of the novel. The lawyer was satisfied. I clamped my teeth on the pipe and rubbed my hands hard. "All right, now. What can you gentlemen tell me about the party slate? I don't know the candidates, but I'm assuming there must be a couple of interesting speakers at least."

"You believe in all that, sir?" asked João Nogueira.

"In what?"

"Elections, deputies, senators."

I checked myself, unsure, because I don't really hold firm ideas on those things. "People get used to whatever they see. And for as long as I can recall, what I've seen are voters and ballot boxes. Sometimes voters and ballot boxes vanish and election results are made up. But it's good for citizens to think they have influence over the government, even if they don't. Up at the ranch, the lowliest worker is convinced that, if he were to abandon his post, everything would grind to a halt. I encourage that illusion. All of them have a stake in it."

João Nogueira considered for a moment. "What I think is that the deputies and senators are useless. They eat too much."

I was going to respond, but I noticed that Sr. Magalhães was stirring uneasily. My response stuck in my throat. He restrained himself, and we played this game for a minute, each of us waiting for the other. I noticed then that the blond girl had turned her big blue eyes on us.

All of a sudden, I realized I was falling for the girl—exactly the opposite of the woman I'd been going around imagining, but she pleased me, dammit. Tiny, weak. Dona Marcela was a stunner: big breasts, big behind, and the nape of her neck!

The silence lengthened. Half speaking to the little blond, I replied to Nogueira. "We hang on to useless things. I hang on to this pipe, even though it's useless and makes me sick." I filled the pipe. "To be frank, though, I'm not positive it's useless. What if it turns out it's not? That's why I go to the elections. You certainly don't want to get rid of the law, sir."

Judge Magalhães, who lived and breathed the law, was scandalized. "Oh!"

"No," returned João Nogueira. "Though laws issued by congress typically aren't worth much. What would be good is to get rid of congress. Laws should be made by specialists."

"Ah," Sr. Magalhães sighed, relieved. Laws or decrees, as long they were printed on paper, were all the same to him. He crossed his legs, nodded his head, frowned, and lifted a finger. "What we need is an elite."

"Exactly," João Nogueira concurred. "An oligarchy."

But Magalhães balked at this term. "Ah! No."

"Come on!" João Nogueira exclaimed. "We can only have an elite of a few individuals in government—an oligarchy."

"But what does the opposition do other than bellowing in the newspapers and in meetings against that?" I asked.

"The opposition doesn't know what it's talking about. Do we have an oligarchy? No, we have a gang of gold diggers. The congressmen alone! And then there are ministers, presidents, governors, secretaries, and the southern politicians. A lot of teeth chomping on the treasure box. Thugs! Look at our representatives in the federal congress. What do you say, Sr. Magalhães?

Magalhães didn't say anything. "I never follow politics. I'm only a judge. I study, consult my books. I wake early, drink a cup of coffee, a small one, shave, shower. Afterward, I take a walk in my garden, return, occupy myself with magazines, and eat lunch, a small one, on account of my stomach. I rest for an hour, write, consult with scholars. I have dinner, take a stroll through the city. At night, I have my friends in, if they come by. I go to sleep."

Dona Glória couldn't restrain herself. "A prudent routine—it's necessary to look after one's health."

João Nogueira had a roguish expression on his face. "Necessary. No doubt. But, as we were saying, we've never had an oligarchy. Too many people."

"But if such a big opposition makes this much noise, imagine if it were smaller. The shouting would never stop."

"Why?"

"Because so many of those on top now would be at the bottom."

The lawyer had come close to the window, so I whispered in his ear. "Did he promise the ruling?"

João Nogueira confirmed this with a sign. I said my goodbyes. "I don't agree with you, Sr. Nogueira. The republic's doing just fine. Our justice system alone ... think about it."

"As for me, I'm just a judge," said Magalhães. "I study, I consult the best writers ..."

I lingered until he had finished, then repeated my goodbyes and left.

I wandered around the city, wasting time, dazzled by the blond girl's eyes and hoping by chance to learn her name.

No luck. I decided to ask João Nogueira for her name, position, family, all the information I'd need to make a serious move. At ten o'clock, I went to the editorial office of the *Cruzeiro*. The only one there was Arquimedes, setting type.

I went to Sousa's pool hall. One customer, half-drunk.

"Sr. Nogueira should be at Ernestina's house."

I didn't know where Ernestina's house was. Around midnight, I found the lawyer at the hotel, debating poetry with Azevedo Gondim. I listened for an hour, hoping to get educated. I didn't.

"Sr. Nogueira—do me a favor? Just a second, Gondim."

But I was too shy to touch on my delicate topic, afraid I'd make a fool of myself. What if Nogueira was carrying his own torch for the blond? Annoyed with myself, I asked for every last detail of the Pereira case.

13

TURNED out I met the blond again. I was on my way back from the capital, where I'd gone on account of that miscreant Brito.

Things unfolded like this. After my telegram (remember: the one where I refused to give that pirate two hundred milreis), the *Gazeta* started libeling me. At first, the pieces were anonymous—sour but beating around the bush. Then the attacks got more direct, including two furious articles where the sweetest name Brito called me was "murderer." When I read this slander, I grabbed a horsewhip and headed down to the city.

"What you need to do is sue," Jōao Nogueira advised. "It'd be easy to get him thrown in jail."

"And if you want to defend yourself, take advantage of the *Cruzeiro*, right here." Azevedo Gondim inserted. "You could write something. Or I could, or Nogueira. Unfortunately, the *Cruzeiro* has a small circulation. But it's what we've got and it's at your disposal."

"Thanks, Gondim. Thanks, Sr. Nogueira. We'll work it out afterward. It's not worth banging your head over such rot."

We lingered at the hotel until eleven that night, playing dominoes for a tostão a point.

Next day, I caught the train, slept like a log, and woke at

ten o'clock in the central station. Horsewhip under my arm, I started scrutinizing faces, then and there.

I went up Comércio Street, made a sharp turn onto Livramento, proceeded up to Alegria, and stopped in front of the *Gazeta*. I peered through the bars at the filthy crates before entering and crossing through the typesetting and printing rooms. At the very back, I emerged in the newsroom, where a single sallow guy was writing headlines based on day-old papers from Recife. He told me the director had taken off for Pajuçara.

"Thanks."

I retraced my steps and spent an hour under the town clock, watching passengers on trams from Ponta-da-Terra. Finally, that rat Brito poked his muzzle out of one.

"Hello!"

He backed up and tried to jump back on the running board, but the streetcar had already left him far behind. He furrowed his brow with dignity. Seeing the horsewhip, he blanched and stammered, "How good to see you. What luck! Yessir, we sure need to talk."

I grabbed hold of his arm, pulling him over next to the clock. Not wanting to alarm passersby, I whispered, "You son of a bitch. Those articles—"

"Paid content," Brito explained. "In the open section, didn't you see? Come to the newsroom—we'll be able to talk better there."

My reply was to sink my talons into the scruff of his neck. I whipped him. A crowd gathered. A security guard whistled. There were shouts of protest. Finally, he slipped my grasp and bolted up Comércio, toward Martírios.

I made my way back to the hotel, but didn't even have time for lunch before I was called down to the police station, where they asked the same questions over and over. I missed my three o'clock train and never even proved to the commissioner that he was just grumpy and stupid. Sick and tired of it, I called a lawyer (three hundred milreis, not to mention taxi, tips, and all the other minor expenses) and only got away twenty-four hours later, a sermon from the Secretary of the Interior ringing in my ears. He'd pumped me full of the freedom of the press and other crap.

On the train, I bought the daily papers. Not one mentioned the brawl—kind of them. I read an interesting piece on beekeeping. Little by little I forgot the commissioner's brainlessness and the secretary's liberalism. I forgave Brito, admitting to myself that he had a good heart and probably wouldn't reoffend. I concentrated on reading. Bees—could be a fountain of wealth.

A lady dressed in black seated herself next to me. The sun was bothering her so I lowered the shutter.

"Much appreciated."

Getting a proper look, I recognized her as the woman who'd sat through Dona Marcela's novel last month, at Judge Magalhães's house. "It's no bother, Dona Glória."

She had a package tearing open on her sharp knees, so I asked if I could put it up with my baggage. She was a shy old thing: a weak smile, the manners of the poor. The train started moving, and we started a conversation that got more and more lively. Soon we were friends.

"The Great Western is a mess. Filthy! This isn't a carriage. It's a pigpen!" I liked starting train journeys with remarks like this. Dona Glória was startled, fearful that somebody close by might overhear. Confidentially, she expressed the view that things could be better.

"Couldn't be worse, Dona Glória."

She studied me. "I believe we've seen each other before. I'm not sure, though. My memory is pitiful."

"At the judge's house, last month, ma'am. You and a blond girl—"

"Ah!" she widened her eyes. "Yes."

The conversation collapsed. To revive it, I opened the newspaper. Pointing a finger, I said, "This is some article, on beekeeping. The writer's got chops."

She didn't get it. Suddenly, she exclaimed, "Now I recall, sir. You were with Sr. Nogueira, discussing politics."

"Exactly."

There was a pause.

"Do you live in the capital, sir?"

"No. In the interior."

"In Viçosa?"

"That's right."

"I do too, or I have for the last little while. Such a small city…horrible, isn't it?"

"Small cities? And big ones. They're all horrible. I like the country, get it? The country."

Dona Glória covered her face. "The backwoods? Heavens! The backwoods are for beasts, sir! You live in the backwoods?"

"At São Bernardo."

Dona Glória didn't know São Bernardo. Her ignorance offended me since for me São Bernardo was the most important place in the world.

"It's a fine ranch. None of that rotten water they drink around here. Mud. No, ma'am, it's comfortable, it's clean."

Dona Glória sat up straight and raised her voice, shaking off her mincing tone. "It wouldn't do for me. I was born and raised in the city. When I'm away, I'm like a fish out of water.

So much so that I've been trying to secure a transfer to a school in the capital. But you need pull. Promises, promises..."

"Ah! You're a teacher?"

"No, my niece is a teacher."

"That girl who was with you at Sr. Magalhães's house, ma'am?"

"Yes."

"And, Dona Glória, what's your niece's name, if I may ask?"

"Madalena. Listen, sir, she was a brilliant student—"

"Wait right there. Nogueira and Gondim spoke to me about her. An accomplished woman, pretty. That's it. Gondim said a lot of things. Gondim, of the *Cruzeiro*, with the snub nose."

"I know," she said, smiling to hear her niece praised. "But a girl like that hidden away in a hole, Sr...."

"Paulo Honório, Dona Glória. Such a shame. Teaching the ABCs. Ridiculous! Pardon my indiscretion, but what does your niece earn for teaching the ABCs?"

Dona Glória lowered her voice and confided that primary school teachers make only one hundred and eighty milreis.

"How much?"

"One hundred and eighty milreis."

"One hundred and eighty milreis! That's it? My good lady, what a disgrace. How the devil is a Christian supposed to keep body and soul together on one hundred and eighty milreis a month? Know what I say? It's enough to enrage you, seeing persons of your class treated so miserably. I have completely uneducated employees who make more than that. Why don't you tell your niece to get out of that line of work, Dona Glória?"

Dona Glória talked about how hard it was to find a job and also about the widow's pension.

"Widow's pension? What? That's not worth a thing. And a job... Ma'am, let me tell you how you and your niece can get rich. Raising chickens."

Dona Glória was offended, and when I went on shouting enthusiastically, the passenger beside her began to laugh. He was a young fellow with a little mustache and a ruby ring. I brought my hairy face and hairy hand up close. "You're laughing without knowing what you're laughing at, sir. I'll bet you've got a diploma. How much does that get you? If you don't have a rich father, you'll end up a public prosecutor. You'd be better off raising chickens."

The young man was embarrassed.

"It's a good living, Dona Glória, a decent living. If you decide to go into it, I recommend Orpingtons. School? Hogwash. I opened one on my ranch and trusted it to Padilha. Do you know who he is? An idiot. But he says there's been progress. And I believe it. At least, when Gondim and Padre Silvestre went in there to check up on the kids, they said everything's in order."

Dona Glória wrinkled and unwrinkled her face. "To each his own."

"Nonsense! Come on by São Bernardo and I'll show you a farm to make your mouth water."

To be clear, our conversation didn't unfold top to tail the way it does on paper. There were pauses, repetitions, misunderstandings, inconsistencies, all natural when people speak without thinking that what they say might be read. I've reproduced whatever I thought was interesting. I left out certain parts and changed others. The speech I fired at the young fellow with the ruby, for example, was more powerful and longer than the drab lines you have here. The part about Dona Glória's migraine (the migraine, no exaggeration, took up half the trip) went up in smoke. I also cut, in my fine copy, a lot of rot both Dona Glória and I said. There's still a lot, though—parts I didn't quite catch at the time and others that seemed useful. This was the process that I decided on: to extract portions of events and dump the rest. See here: when I dragged Costa Brito over to the town clock, I employed some four or five obscene swear words. These swear words were unnecessary because they neither increased nor decreased the value of the whipping. They vanished, as will be noted by those who have read that violent scene—a scene which, profanities cut, is presented with considerable gravity.

One thing I left out that would have produced a good effect was the landscape. I did wrong. My story reads like a lecture delivered far away from the earth. Let me explain: there, with the shutter closed, I could only glimpse, through other windows, bits of stations, bits of forest, factories, and cane fields. Lots of cane fields, but that type of agriculture doesn't interest me. I also saw zebu calves—a breed of cattle that, in my opinion, is well on its way to ruining our herds.

Today it's all one big muddle for me. If I tried to describe it, I'd probably mix up the coconuts by the lagoon, which appeared at three fifteen, with the mango and cashew trees that came later. Anyway, I'd only be sticking the description in here for technical reasons. I don't have a writing scheme that conforms to rules. To prove this, I'm going to make a mistake. I assume it's a mistake. I'm going to divide one chapter into two. Really, what's about to follow might fit better into whatever I tried to explain before my digression. But rest assured, I'm making a chapter specially for Madalena.

14

AT THE station, Dona Glória introduced me to the niece, who had come to pick her up. I got flustered and, freeing my hand, dropped one of the packages I was going to give the porter.

"A great pleasure, miss. I already knew you by name. And by sight. But I didn't know that both were one and the same person. We met each other a few days ago."

"It's been a month."

"Exactly. I was just saying that to your aunt, who was a marvelous traveling companion. Yes, ma'am, what a pleasure."

I headed toward the hotel. Their house was on my way, so we went together.

"Dona Marcela told me that you have a charming estate, sir," Madalena began.

"Charming? Not that I've noticed. Maybe it's charming. It's a well-run estate, that's for certain." I clammed up, bashful. Up to now my feelings had been simple, rudimentary. There was no reason to hide them with creatures like Germana and Rosa. I tossed them lines without beating around the bush, and they never thought twice about it, but a lady who went to teachers' college is different. Stuck, I brooded, counted the bundles balanced on the porter's head, forced myself to extend courtesies to Dona Glória. "The invitation stands, Dona Glória, and I have your promise that you will come and spend a few days at the ranch. I hope you will bring the teacher. Come by car—you'll be there in ten minutes." Dona Glória hadn't promised anything.

Madalena was surprised. "Ah! No."

"Why? Now with the holidays..."

"Excursions...That's for the rich." Smiling, she added, "What would your family say if you had two strange women in your house?"

Now it was my turn to be surprised. "But I have no family, my good lady, I never did. I live alone, with God."

"So it's worse," Madalena responded.

"Improper," Dona Glória declared.

I scratched my beard. "That's a shame. It's such a good place for a person to rest up! Over and done with: if it's improper, let's say it was never said." Then I changed my mind. "But how's it improper? Especially since I'd love to show Dona Glória my Peking ducks, really, things of beauty. Have you ever seen Peking ducks, Dona Madalena?"

"Not yet."

"There you go!" I muttered. "You can study your whole life without knowing what for."

We were at the door of their house, in Canafístula. "Will you stop in, rest up for a minute?" said Dona Glória.

"Thank you, but I should be getting along to the hotel." I lingered a minute more. "You ladies deserve better than digs like these. So long. If you decide to come to São Bernardo, let me know so I can send the car."

"Lovely," said Dona Glória. "Much obliged for the company."

"It's nothing at all."

At the hotel, I marched straight to the bath and got rid of the soot and sweat. I was about to sit down to supper when

João Nogueira, Azevedo Gondim, and Padre Silvestre arrived.

"So what was all the commotion?" asked Azevedo Gondim. "We learned about it last night."

"Think how shocked we were," added the vicar. "A scandal! It's true that Brito did wrong."

"He did. It was necessary. It's not that he's so bad. He wanted two hundred milreis, poor sod, and I turned him down. What garbage: I spent a good six hundred, not counting two days of aggravation. The hell of it is, if he had gotten the two hundred, he'd have asked for two hundred more and so on."

"Yesterday the news was that he was in the hospital with a stab wound," Padre Silvestre informed me. "The story was he was close to death. Fortunately, things have calmed down. Lightly injured, was he?"

"What injuries? We traded words, that's all. Brito insulted me, I replied, people gathered around, and the police got involved, even though it was none of their business. Nothing happened."

"I see that now," exclaimed Padre Silvestre. "A prudent gentleman such as yourself would never provoke a disturbance."

"Come on!" shouted Azevedo Gondim. "I've already written two columns about the case for the Sunday edition."

João Nogueira came close to me and spoke under his breath. "Honestly, what happened?"

"An insignificant dispute." But, seizing the occasion, I asked, "Say, Sr. Nogueira, who is that Dona Glória?"

"The teacher's aunt?"

"Yeah. What's the family like?"

"In what sense?"

"In every sense," I answered evasively. "The old lady traveled with me today, on the train. She was pleasant."

"But what sort of interest do you have, sir..."

"Just that the woman, indirectly, made a request to have her niece transferred. I don't know the Director of Public Education, but I'm acquainted with Silveira, in Policy. Maybe a transfer wouldn't be impossible. If it's deserved, of course."

"But she's an excellent teacher, Sr. Paulo, with upright character. And you want to pull her out! What a suggestion! If she leaves, you know what will happen? They'll send out some illiterate old lady."

"Good point." In a normal voice, I asked, "Supper?"

They all begged off. Padre Silvestre embraced me. "My friend in a scrape like this! It's Brito's fault. He's a hothead, but lately he's been taking the *Gazeta* in a good direction."

I walked with them. "Say, Gondim, I need to talk to you." He stayed back. "I'm dying of hunger, Gondim. Two whole days and hardly a bite to eat. Just think. Come have supper?"

He declined supper, but accepted a beer. By the time I got to dessert, he was on his third bottle.

"Say, Gondim, you talked to me a while ago about a teacher."

"Madalena?"

"Yes. I met her one night recently and I liked her face. Is she an honorable girl?"

Azevedo Gondim swallowed a quarter-bottle of beer and fell all over himself praising her. "A superior woman. Her articles in the *Cruzeiro* alone!"

I was discouraged. "Ah! She writes articles!"

"Yes, sir, she's very learned. What have you got to do with her?"

"No idea. I had a plan, but the *Cruzeiro* contributions give me cold feet. I'd assumed she was sensible."

"Come on, sir!" Gondim cried, piqued. "If it's not one thing it's another!"

"All right. I've got no secrets from you. Listen. I'm fed up with Padilha."

"Bingeing again?"

"Worse. He's bringing socialism to the ranch. I caught him spouting bullshit. I didn't make much of it, kept him on, but the more I think about it, the better it might be to find him some other position, far away."

"And invite Madalena."

"Yeah, that's what I was thinking. I don't know. If she's a girl of good habits."

"Good habits? Of course. The hell of it is she might not accept. Life out in the boondocks!"

"That's her aunt's garbage. Silly old lady. But the other one, if she's got sense, as you say, she'd accept."

Azevedo Gondim munched roasted peanuts and drank beer. "Sure, could be. It'd be to her advantage, certainly, increase her salary."

"No doubt."

"Could be. I just feel sorry for that poor Padilha."

"No, I'll dig up some position for him. Didn't I just say so? He's a fink, pathetic. Regarding the girl..."

"Do you have an understanding with her, sir?"

"No, man. If I had an understanding, I wouldn't be asking your advice. Say, Gondim, do me a favor. I asked you to stay back specifically for this. Sound the woman out."

Azevedo Gondim resisted, exaggerating the help he'd be giving me. "But I hardly know her. You talk with her, sir."

"Impossible. I've been away for two days. I need to get to São Bernardo today. And I don't know how to behave with folks like that, talking in circles. Do me a favor, Gondim: entice the girl."

"All right. I'll paint a picture of the countryside, the poetry of the fields, the simple souls. And if she's not convinced, I'll sprinkle a handful of patriotism on top."

15

AFTER the invitation, I got to know the women a little better. Madalena took her time deciding. On the pretext of wanting an answer, I starting dropping by their little house in Canafístula. One day, I felt out Dona Glória. "Why doesn't your niece get married?"

She was offended. "My niece isn't day-old bread on offer for whoever will take her."

"I never said that, good lady. God help me. It's advice from a friend. A guarantee for her future . . ."

Dona Glória sat up, flattening her sunken chest. This sudden, dignified movement made her black dress, already shabby, stretch across her stomach and droop across her back. She muttered inaudibly, until, little by little, she returned to her usual position, her shoulder blades conforming to the threadbare fabric. Her gargling became intelligible. "Marriage for women . . . is seen as . . . a situation . . ."

"It's quite sensible, Dona Glória. Even good for the health."

"But there are so many disastrous marriages . . . Above all, it's not something that can be forced."

"No, unfortunately. There's got to be a proposal. It's all badly organized, Dona Glória. How can anybody know who they should marry?"

"As far as I'm concerned, in romantic matters, reciprocity is crucial."

"Reciprocity? What fuss. If the couple's good, the children come out good; bad, and the children won't amount to much. The parents' wishes don't mean much one way or another. So says my domestication and breeding manual."

After this conversation, the cotton harvest kept me at São Bernardo for two weeks. I reflected on the situation from time to time. Dona Glória had to be flapping her jaws. What was she saying? I went over to Madalena's, worried I'd be unwelcome on account of my suggestion. I was welcomed.

"How's the farming coming along?"

"It's going as it should. I think it's going as it should: I can't yet tell what the harvest's going to yield. And your school? The children, Dona Glória, any news? I'm interested. I'm pretty sure that you don't care much about farming, miss, and I came to talk about another subject."

"The invitation you made to me via Gondim?"

I vacillated. "More or less."

"I should have already responded that I'm not accepting."

"Dammit! What about the increase in salary, for God's sake?"

"It didn't convince me. I've been teaching for six years. I don't want to trade a sure thing for a dubious one. These private schools open one day and close the next..."

I complimented her. "I commend you on your prudence. You'd risk ending up without the honey or the calabash."

"Sir, if you can appreciate—"

"Oh, I appreciate. I'm here with another proposal, to be honest—the tale of the school was a sham."

Madalena waited, a tiny pucker between her eyebrows.

"It's hard to say what I need to. You have to understand... Anyway, so we don't get stuck in preambles, I'll lay down my bundle and speak with my heart in my hand." I coughed, befuddled. "Look, here. I need a companion. And, well, you suit me, miss . . . Yes, I took a liking to you, miss, the first time I saw you . . ." I choked.

Serious and pale, Madalena stayed quiet but didn't appear surprised.

"I know I'm not the perfect man that you have in your head."

She dismissed this remark with a slim hand, long fingers. "It's not that. It's just that we don't know each other."

"Listen to this! Haven't I told you things about my life? What I haven't told you isn't worth much. And from what I've seen and heard, miss, you're judicious and thrifty. You know which way the wind blows, and you'd make a good mother."

Madalena went to the window and leaned out, watching the street for a time. When she returned, I was walking around the room, filling my pipe.

"I suspect we're very different."

"Different? So? If we weren't, we'd be the same person. Of course we're different. Beg pardon, I'm going to light my pipe. You've learned about certain kinds of strife by going to school, I've learned about other kinds banging my head against this world. I'm forty-five, and you're barely twenty."

"No, twenty-seven."

"Twenty-seven? No one would put you a day over twenty. But there you go. We're closer already. With a sprinkling of goodwill, we'll be in church in a week."

"Your offer is flattering to me, Sr. Paulo Honório," Madalena murmured. "Very flattering. But I still need to think on it. Regardless, I'm obliged to you, sir. Do you hear? The truth is I'm poor as Job, do you understand?"

"Don't talk like that, girl. Your education, your person, aren't these worth anything? Want to know what I say? If we come to an agreement, I'll be getting the better bargain by far."

16

EARLY afternoon a week later, I was having coffee at the house on Canafístula, chatting and feeling smug at having been installed there since midday. Then, in the best part of the conversation, Azevedo Gondim burst in and made a colossal gaffe. "Ah! You're here? I came to offer my congratulations to Dona Madalena. So glad to see you here, sir. My best wishes."

"What sort of tale is this?" I asked, trembling.

"The wedding," Azevedo Gondim explained. "Everybody's talking about it. You never said anything, sir! When is it?"

I didn't say anything. Madalena counted embroidery threads. Dona Glória was paralyzed, a cup in her hand. I fought an urge to wring Gondim's neck. He realized his folly, backing up against a wall and rubbing his chin. I got up and moved to the window to hide my mortification. Gondim came over to me and I growled, "Are you drunk?"

"I didn't think it was secret. Everyone knows."

"Idiot."

I returned to my seat. Embarrassed, my ears burning, I seized on the Our Lady of Conception Hospital and the Literary and Recreational Guild, which led a precarious existence, bookshelves full of wormholes, opening once a year for the board of directors. "What use is it?"

Azevedo Gondim sat down, calming down little by little. "It's a society that does good work, Sr. Paulo."

"Lies! The hospital, yessir. But a library in a place like this? For what? For Nogueira to read a novel once a month. Worthless publications..."

Once he gets hold of an idea, Azevedo Gondim circles round it like a turkey. "Education is indispensable. Education is key. Don't you agree, Dona Madalena?"

"A person accustomed to books—"

I interrupted. "Don't get accustomed to them, and you won't confuse education with reading a printed page."

"They're the same," Gondim said.

"Not a bit!"

"And how can you get educated if not by books?"

"Out in the world—looking, listening, running around. Nogueira was learned as the devil when he graduated, but he didn't know how to interrogate a witness. Today he's forgotten his Latin and turned into a good lawyer."

"Regardless, you think the hospital is necessary, sir. And why don't you throw out your agricultural treatises?"

"That's different. I suspect doctors learn less from books than they do by opening stomachs, cutting up bodies, dead or alive, doing experiments. In any case, in my spare time, I only read what practitioners have to say and I don't even value that overmuch—I trust myself over anyone else. Those authors haven't come and seen São Bernardo's lands up close."

Madalena nodded. "Exactly. The thing is, we're not used to thinking like that. I recently saw a film at the cinema, and I believe I learned more than if I'd seen it written down. Not to mention it took less time."

"And you don't pack your nut with straw," I added. "You

guys swallow a lot of stuff and nonsense, Gondim. There are whole volumes in there that could have been four lines long."

Dona Glória was nearly asleep. Azevedo Gondim, baffled and vexed, shrugged. "For me, books are useful. But if you think they're useless, sir, you must have your reasons."

"You know I'm referring to those tall tales at the Society."

"What's harder is that something unnecessary to you might well be necessary for many," said Madalena.

"Without doubt. Beauty," crowed Azevedo Gondim. "That's what they want. Harmony, beauty, you understand?"

"Give me a break!"

Dona Glória got up and went inside. The topic had been reduced to ashes and we quieted down. Pointlessly, Azevedo Gondim tried to stir up the embers. "How about this dust, then? With the northeaster and all."

He left.

I gathered my courage and moved next to Madalena. "See? They're already talking out there. It's all they're talking about, according to Gondim." No response. "I'm not setting foot in here again. First, because I don't want to influence you, miss, and secondly because it's ridiculous. Of course, you must have already thought it over."

Madalena tossed aside her embroidery. "It appears we understand each other. I always wanted to live in the country, get up early, have a garden. There is a garden there, right? But why can't you wait just a little longer? To be honest, I'm not in love."

"Come on! If you'd said you were, I wouldn't have believed you. Anyway, I don't like it when people fall in love with each other and do things blindly. Especially things like this. Let's set a day."

"There's no rush. Perhaps a year from now? I need to prepare myself."

"A year? An agreement that comes due in a year doesn't even count. What do you need? A white dress can be made in twenty-four hours." Hearing footsteps in the hall, I lowered my voice. "We should tell your aunt, shouldn't we?"

She smiled hesitantly. "All right, then."

"Have you finished with the heavy debate yet?" asked Dona Glória from the door. "I was nodding off."

"Me too. It was Gondim's fault, with his fancy ideas."

I tried to find a way to put it, but I got all worked up and tongue-tied. "Dona Glória, I would like to inform you that, within a week, your niece and I are getting hitched. To use more proper language, we will marry. Obviously, you'll come with us, ma'am. Where two can eat, so can three. And the house is large, with nooks to tuck you away in."

Dona Glória started to cry.

17

PADRE Silvestre married us in São Bernardo's chapel, in front of the altar of São Pedro.

It was the end of January. The pau d'arcos, in flower, peppered the woods with yellow points; the mountains smoked in the morning; the creek gurgled, swollen by recent storms. It played at being a river and, where it crashed into the waterfall before entering the sluice, adorned itself with foam.

When she saw the electric lights, telephone, furniture, and metal utensils polished to a shine by Maria das Dores, Dona Glória admitted that life here could be bearable.

"Didn't I say so?"

I offered her a room on the left side of the house, behind the study, with a window facing the church's red wall. Today that wall is greenish from rainwater, but back then it was new, the color of raw meat. Madalena and I stayed on the right side: from our veranda, we could see the cotton fields, the meadow, the cotton gin with the lumber mill, and the road, which curved around a hill.

"We're starting a new life, aren't we?" Madalena said joyfully.

From then on, I began to make discoveries about her that took me by surprise. As you know, I had been satisfied with her face and a few superficial inquiries. For a week, I worked on cleaning up my syntax but made plenty of mistakes anyway. I changed tack. That was all nonsense. Madalena didn't care about those things. I'd imagined she was a well-educated doll. I was wrong. Padilha, who she thought a "low character," made her sick. (I explained that his character didn't matter: forget the rest, I need my men to work.) He made her sick. But she liked Sr. Ribeiro. She inserted herself into the study, flipped through the books, examined documents, dismantled the jammed typewriter. Two days after the wedding, still with a wounded air about her, she took off toward the fields and tore her skirt on the cotton stalks. At lunchtime, I found her at the cotton gin, chatting with the operator.

"Well, now. That's women for you." I told her not to make a spectacle of herself. "These mestizos are brutes. You want to work? I'll arrange it. Work with Maria das Dores. Leave the farm folk to me."

"Maria das Dores's jobs don't suit me. And I didn't come here to sleep."

"Whims."

"Another thing," Madalena continued. "Mestre Caetano's family is suffering hardship."

"You've already met Mestre Caetano?" I asked, astonished. "Hardship—always the same old song. Truth is, I don't need him anymore. It'd be better for him to go look for a living somewhere else."

"He's ill . . ."

"He should have saved. They're all like that, shortsighted. They get sick and that's it: advances on pay and on medicines, and there goes my profit."

"He's already worked too much! And he's so old!"

"Sure is. And weak. He wedges a crowbar under a tiny

stone and has to get the quarrymen to move it. He's not worth the six milreis he's getting. But don't you worry, I'll send him whatever he needs—a half-measure of wheat, a few liters of beans. Money down the drain."

18

"You, EXCELLENT lady," Sr. Ribeiro declared, "understand accounting."

Sr. Ribeiro lived here and worked with me, but he didn't like me. I don't believe he liked anybody. Everything about him still looked back toward the hamlet that had since turned into a city but that—half a century ago—had had a sugar mill, rosaries, oil lamps, and fortune tellers on São João festival nights. Though he was over seventy years old, he walked everywhere, especially on the footpaths. The telephone made him nervous. He hated the era he lived in, but he dealt with it by using old-fashioned manners and expressions. What little warmth he had was lavished on those big books with copper corners and spines. He would lovingly write complicated entries in them, spending fifteen minutes making new headings—large, curved, and a little shaky, with initial letters heavily embellished.

"You understand plenty," he continued. "And although I don't wholly agree with the method you extol, I acknowledge that you could, if you wished, assume command of it."

"Thank you."

"Gratitude is hardly in order. The excellent lady knows the subject and has beautiful penmanship. I'm a relic. One of these days . . ." He searched for the words. "One of these days, I shall be with God."

"You always say that," Padilha grumbled. "But you're strong as an ox." His ambition was to take over both teaching and bookkeeping, and he was getting impatient.

"I am no longer hale and hearty. I am spent," Sr. Ribeiro responded. "And I would die at peace if I were leaving the books with a person who would not ruin them with deletions."

"Easy work," Padilha muttered.

"Maybe, but some knowledge would make it go better. Her grace here . . ."

"That's a good one," Padila retorted. "Dona Madalena writing stuff about stuff."

"Nothing would be more natural," Madalena interrupted. "Not that I wish for it, God help me. Sr. Ribeiro is strong."

"We're all mortal, my good lady. It is true that none can know the mind of Providence, but at my age . . ."

"What's the salary?"

Padilha found this strange. "Come on! The lady troubling herself over scraps? Receiving a salary? That'd be taking from one hand to put it in the other."

"Why not? If Sr. Ribeiro has to retire . . . sir, Sr. Ribeiro, how much do you make?"

The accountant stroked his white whiskers. "Two hundred milreis."

Madalena was discouraged. "So little."

"Come again?" I cried, trembling.

"It's very little."

"Lunacy! When he was with Brito, he earned one hundred and fifty, no extras. Now he gets two hundred, room, board, and laundry."

"That's correct," Sr. Ribeiro admitted. "I want for nothing, and what I receive suffices."

"If you had ten children, sir, it wouldn't suffice," Madalena said.

"True," Dona Glória agreed.

"What crap!" I bellowed. "You too, ma'am? Stick to your novels."

Madalena blanched. "You don't need to get angry. We all have our opinions."

"No doubt. But this is ridiculous, people having opinions on things they know nothing about. Each monkey on his own branch. What the hell. I don't go around debating grammar, but I'm pretty sure I know best how to run my ranch. It'd be nice if you didn't come around giving me lessons. You're all making me lose my patience."

I threw my napkin onto my plate, even before dessert, and got up. A quarrel eight days after the wedding. Bad sign. But I blamed Dona Glória, though she'd only said one word.

19

MADALENA was good to a fault, I knew, though I didn't see it right away. She revealed herself little by little, and never completely. I'm to blame, or maybe I should say this rough life is. It gave me a rough soul.

I'm wasting time, talking like this, I realize. If I can't grasp my wife's character, what's this story for? Nothing, but I still have to write it.

The crickets sing as I sit here at the dining room table, drink coffee, light my pipe. Sometimes no ideas come, sometimes too many—but the page remains half-written, just like yesterday. I reread some lines. They're not good enough, but it's not worth it to try to fix them. I push the paper aside.

Vague emotions stir in me—a terrible turmoil, a crazy desire to go back, to talk once more with Madalena, as we did every day at this hour. Nostalgia? No, it's not that. It's desperation, rage, an enormous weight on my heart.

I try to recall what we said. Impossible. My words were just words, imperfect reproductions of exterior facts, and hers had something about them I can't express. To feel them, I used to switch off the lights, letting shadows envelop us until we were two indistinct figures in the darkness.

Outside, the toads declaimed, the wind moaned, the trees in the orchard lost their outlines in the dark.

"Casimiro!"

Casimiro Lopes was in the garden, squatting under the window, keeping watch.

"Casimiro!"

His shape appears in the window, the toads scream, the wind tosses the trees, barely visible in the gloom. Maria das Dores comes in, meaning to flip the switch. I stop her: I don't want light.

The tick-tock of the clock fades, the crickets begin to sing again. And Madalena appears on the other side of the table. I say softly, "Madalena!"

Her voice reaches my ears. No, not my ears. Nor am I seeing her with my eyes.

I lean on the table, my hands crossed. Objects melt together, and I can't make out the white tablecloth.

"Madalena..."

Madalena's voice continues caressing me. What's she saying? Of course: she's asking me to send some money to Mestre Caetano. It irritates me, but this irritation is different from the others, an old irritation that leaves me utterly calm. Crazy for a person to be angry and calm at the same time, but that's how I am. Irritated at who? At Mestre Caetano. Never mind that he's dead, he better get to work. Lazybones!

The tablecloth reappears, but I don't know if it's the tablecloth I've crossed my hands on or the one that was here five years ago.

A sudden racket of wind, of toads, of crickets. The door of the study opens slowly, and Sr. Ribeiro's footsteps move away. An owl hoots in the church tower. Is that really an owl's hoot? Could it be the same owl that hooted two years ago? Perhaps. It could even be the same hoot.

Now Sr. Ribeiro is talking with Dona Glória in the living room. I forget that they left me and that this house is practically deserted.

"Casimiro!"

I believe I called Casimiro Lopes. His head in its leather cowboy hat looms from time to time at the window, but I can't tell if the vision is from now or long ago.

Irreconcilable emotions surge up in me, infuriate and stir me. I pound the table and want to cry.

To all appearances, I'm tranquil: hands still crossed on the tablecloth and fingers like stone. Meanwhile, I threaten Madalena with my fist. Strange.

In the ranch's drone, I make out the most minute things. Maria das Dores giving the parrot lessons in the kitchen. Shark growling yonder in the garden. The cattle lowing in the stable.

The living room is far away, down a long hall, yet Sr. Ribeiro and Dona Glória's conversation is quite clear. Not that I can tell what they're saying. They're speaking without words.

Padilha is whistling on the porch. Wherever had Padilha gone?

If I could convince Madalena that she's wrong... If I could explain to her that we have to live in peace... She doesn't understand me. We don't understand each other. What's going to happen will be very different from what we had hoped. Absurd.

There's a vast silence. It's July. The northeaster isn't blowing and the toads are asleep. As for the owls, Marciano climbed up the outside of the church and finished them off with a stick. And the crickets' holes are plugged.

I repeat: All this still torments me.

What I don't make out is the tick-tock of the clock. What time is it? I can't see its face in this darkness. When I sat down here, you could hear the pendulum's strikes, you could hear them very well. I ought to wind the clock, but I can't make myself move.

20

As I said, Madalena had a good heart. I was touched by the marks of tenderness I found in her, and as you know, I'm not easily touched. It's true that I've tried to change in these last two years, but that won't go on forever.

Madalena's acts of kindness surprised me. She was charity itself. Later, I learned these were only traces of the goodwill she felt toward all living beings. Mercy. I shouldn't have hoped for crumbs, and I got a feast. We lived very well for a time.

Remember, I left the table annoyed with Dona Glória. After a few minutes, Madalena brought me a cup of coffee and gave me to understand she felt sorry for provoking the incident.

"It was thoughtless," I said.

"It was," Madalena stammered, blushing, "inconsiderate."

"We should think before we speak."

"Certainly," she said, quite disturbed. "I forgot that those two were employees and I put my foot in my mouth. Oh, it was a blunder and a big one."

At this, I took the cup of coffee and soothed her. "No, it wasn't all that. Why exaggerate? It was just a misunderstanding. Thank you, yes—a little sugar. A misunderstanding, that's the word. Let me explain. Here, it's not like out there. Cinema, bars, invitations, the lottery, billiards, whatever damn thing, we don't have it. Sometimes we don't even know what to spend our money on. Can I tell you something? I started life with a hundred milreis that belonged to someone else. One hundred milreis, yes, ma'am. I stretched them like rubber. Everything I have today came from those hundred milreis that that thief Pereira loaned me—Jewish usury, five percent a month."

Madalena listened attentively, sympathetically, like a well-mannered girl. "I believe it, I believe it. The problem is that I still don't know this way of life. I need to get used to it."

I called for Casimiro Lopes, handed him the cup and tray, and lit my pipe. "What I feel..." I rose. "I never regret anything. What's done is done. After all, a long face never got anyone anywhere. But what I lobbed at Dona Glória..."

"Poor thing. She wasn't even paying attention to the conversation. She was just talking for talking's sake."

"It was just one of those things. Do me a favor. Make her see I had no intention of hurting her. An elderly person, and respectable... I had no intention, you hear? I'm a cranky sort of guy."

As you see, we were as mild as two bananas. And so a month went by. At her insistence, I gave her a job: "Take care of the correspondence. You want a salary? No problem. We'll arrange it later. Sr. Ribeiro will open an account for you."

21

STILL, in spite of our precautions, the insulation we used to absorb the friction, there were clashes, more and more, a lot.

In the morning, Madalena worked in the study, but in the afternoon, she'd go out walking, visiting the tenant workers' houses. Thick-lipped children covered in sores clung to her skirts.

She went to the school, criticized Padilha's teaching methods, and started pestering me for a globe, maps, and other gear I won't list because I don't want to go to the bother of looking it all up in the files. One day, absentmindedly, I ordered what she asked for. When the bill arrived, I started shaking. Due: six thousand milreis. Six thousand for notebooks, cards, and little wooden tablets for the workers' children. Think of it. A man who learned to read in jail with an ABC chart, calendars, and a little black Protestant Bible, spending that kind of money. But I held back. I held back because I'd resolved to get along with my wife and because I imagined showing the paraphernalia to the governor if he ever came around. In any case, it was an uncalled-for expense.

I signed the invoice, put on my hat, and went out. When I passed the stable, I noticed that the animals didn't have any feed.

"This is no good." I shouted, "Marciano!"

I shouted in vain. Enraged, I went down the hill. There

at the bottom, in the schoolhouse doorway, I discovered Marciano, sprawled on a stool, gossiping with Padilha.

"Get back to your duties, you good-for-nothing."

"I finished my work, Sr. Paulo," Marciano stammered, drawing himself up.

"You haven't finished a thing!"

"I finished, sir, yes. I swear, on the Creator's light."

"Liar. The animals are dying of hunger, gnawing on the wood."

Marciano had a fit. "Just now the troughs were full. I've never seen cattle eat so much. No one can stand living on this land anymore. Not a minute's rest."

It was true, but no tenant worker had ever spoken to me in this way. "You spouting bullshit, you worthless son of a bitch?" I clouted him on the ear and knocked him to the ground. He got up reeling, feeble, got five more thumps, and took that many tumbles. The last one left him kicking around in the dust. Finally, he got up and left, head hanging, steps unsteady, wiping his bloody nose on his sleeve. I was out of breath for a few minutes. Then I rounded on Padilha. "You're the culprit."

"Me?"

"Yes, you. Going around filling that loafer full of hot air."

Padilha, pale, defended himself. "I don't go around filling anything, Sr. Paulo, no way. That's unfair. He came and stuck his nose in, believe me. I didn't ask him over. I even said, 'Marciano, you better go feed the animals.' He didn't listen, just stayed here prattling. It made me sick, by God in heaven. I don't like the face on that punk."

I was about to give him a piece of my mind, but I caught sight of Madalena who, standing on the wall of the dam, had turned toward what was left of Marciano.

I went over to them, muttering, "The disrespect! Give them a hand—they want your arm."

But my rage was gone. What was bugging me now were the boxes of educational materials, useless in this backwater. What good were they? The governor would be happy if the school produced a few people capable of registering to vote.

"Getting some fresh air, are you?" Madalena asked, her gaze held by the dark roof of the stable.

I didn't answer but cast a glance over the animals' watering hole, the riverbed, dry apart from the drainage from the dam, and, in the distance, up against the mountains, the quarry, a whitish smudge. The woods were darkening. A cold wind started to blow. The last loads of cotton arrived at the gin. There was a late whistle blast and the laborers left work. I looked at my watch: six o'clock.

"It's horrible!" cried Madalena.

"Come again?"

"Horrible!" she insisted.

"What is?"

"Your conduct! What barbarity! Completely uncalled-for!"

"What the hell—" Was she delirious? No: she seemed lucid, frowning, with a wrinkle between her brows. "I don't understand. Explain yourself."

Her voice trembled with indignation. "What kind of man hits a living creature like that?"

"Oh, right. Marciano. I thought it might be something serious. You startled me."

In that moment I never imagined that such a trivial thing could cause a rift between reasonable people.

"Beating a man like that? How horrible!"

Since this was all silliness, I supposed she was annoyed for some other reason.

"It's a trifle, my girl. You're drowning yourself in a puddle here. These folks follow orders but not without a beating. Marciano's not really a man."

"Why?"

"I have no idea! God's will. He's a milksop."

"Clearly. You spend your life humiliating him."

"I object!" I exclaimed, riled up now. "He was already a milksop when I met him."

"Probably because he'd always been kicked around."

"Fat chance! He's a milksop because he was born a milksop."

Madalena fell silent, turned her back, and started climbing the hill. Sullen, I accompanied her. Suddenly, she turned, her voice hoarse, a flame in her eyes, the blue turned nearly black. "But it's cruel. Why do you do it?"

I lost my temper. "I do it because I think I should, and I'm not in the habit of justifying myself, you hear? That's all I need. Big deal, some hayseed gets shoved a couple of times. What the hell is going on between you and Marciano for you to get so broody over him?"

22

DONA GLÓRIA loved talking with Sr. Ribeiro, endless conversations, in two registers: he spoke loudly and looked straight ahead; she whispered and looked to the sides. Whenever I came by, she fell silent.

I understand these shifts perfectly. I used to be a field hand, and I know it's normal for underlings to spend break time putting down their betters. For Dona Glória these days, break time was all the time.

She'd sleep, eat lunch, eat supper, read novels in the shade of the orange trees, and harass Maria das Dores, driving her crazy with help. She complained about everything: the rats, the toads, the snakes, the dark. Whenever I was around, she played the martyr. She never got tired of boasting about the city for no reason. And she spent part of each day in the study.

Sr. Ribeiro called her "most excellent lady" (Madalena was only "excellent lady"). From certain words, gestures, and silences, I could tell she was bemoaning her niece's fate. She was always standing by the desk, pestering them.

Madalena would be banging on the typewriter. Sr. Ribeiro would be writing, slow and shaky, or peevishly hunting for a ruler, an eraser, a bottle of glue—misplaced because Dona Glória had a bad habit of messing with things, never putting them back where she found them. The chaos drove me crazy.

Stone-faced, I'd give brisk orders and then leave so I wouldn't blow up. I finally let loose. It was the fourth, and the previous month's balance sheet wasn't ready.

"Why are you behind, Sr. Ribeiro? Not feeling well?"

The old man scratched his whiskers, distressed. "No, sir. There's a difference in the totals. I've been trying to find the problem since yesterday, but I can't."

"Why, Sr. Ribeiro?"

He fell silent.

"It's fine. Put a sign on the door forbidding anyone who doesn't have business here to enter. This is our workplace. A sign with nice big letters. Anyone, you hear? No exceptions."

"Is this about me?" Dona Glória said, drawing herself up.

"Make the sign right away, Sr. Ribeiro."

"I asked if this was about me," Dona Glória repeated, shrinking down a little.

"Now, my good lady—it's about everyone. If I say no exceptions, I mean no exceptions."

"I came to talk with my niece," Dona Glória stammered, dwindling back to her normal size.

"Your niece, while she's in this room, isn't receiving guests. She's an employee like everyone else."

"I didn't know. I didn't think I was interrupting."

"You thought wrong. No one can write, calculate, and converse all at the same time."

Dona Glória left, describing a right angle: she stole along the writing desk to the wall, then edged along it to the door, opening and closing it silently. I sat down and started comparing the daily expense log with the account book. Sr. Ribeiro came over to assist me.

"Thank you," I told him.

With a pocketknife and ruler, Sr. Ribeiro cut a square of

cardboard. Madalena got up, covered the typewriter, brought me the letters, waited as I read them, then withdrew. I signed the letters and put them in envelopes.

"What was Dona Glória stirring up in here, Sr. Ribeiro?"

"Nothing of any importance," the accountant responded. "The lady Dona Glória has a heart of gold and discourses proficiently on various themes, but, to be frank, I have not paid sufficient attention."

Ridiculous, I thought, to cross-examine such an earnest man on Dona Glória's intrigues.

"A lady of excellence," Sr. Ribeiro affirmed, marking lines with his pen on the square of cardboard.

"That's one way of putting it." I got up. "Watch out for intruders."

"Absolutely," responded Sr. Ribeiro.

In the living room, I found Madalena, collapsed on the sofa, melancholy. She wiped her eyes hastily. "Why were you such a brute?"

Madalena was pregnant, and I handled her like fine china. Lately, she'd been disagreeable to me, saying things I pretended not to understand. I was watching her belly grow—one compensation. I sat down and, so as to smooth things over, said, "I was a brute. I needed to be, but that doesn't change the fact that I was. It's such a nuisance to have to resort to that."

"So *why* resort to it?" Madalena scoffed.

"Here you go, starting already. For crying out loud, don't do it this way. I hate little digs. Give it to me straight. Blunt. No ploys."

"Who's using ploys? It was brutal."

"It was necessary."

"Unnecessary. It's easy to see that you don't like my aunt."

"Me? I don't like or dislike her. I think she wants a job.

On that topic, it would be better if you stopped using the typewriter. It's bad for your belly. Don't you feel ill?"

"No."

"In any case, you'll get a few months off, both before and after the birth."

"Thank you."

"As I was saying, my guess is that your aunt would like some work. I even gave her some advice about this once, on the train. It offended her. She's got too much time on her hands, reading trash. I don't dislike her. But I don't think it's right for her to get in the way of other people's work."

"Listen, Paulo," Madalena sobbed. "You're mistaken. You're wrong, I swear you're wrong. My aunt is a person of dignity."

"Agreed, she has some kind of dignity, a kind you can see through pretty fast."

Madalena persisted. "I don't know anyone who works more than Dona Glória."

"Come on!" I cried with such astonishment that it raised me off the sofa.

"Are you going out?"

Thinking back on it now, I don't believe it was the astonishment that got me up. More likely it was my habit of walking through the fields every morning. In fact, I wasn't thinking of the farm at all in that moment, but Dona Glória and Madalena had already put me almost an hour behind, and my movement corresponded to a need that only occurred to me once I was on my feet. "Shall we go?"

Madalena came along. As we left, she said, "You told me you yourself started out in life very poor."

"I have no idea how I started out! My earliest memory was of being a guide to a blind man. Then I sold coconut candy for Mother Margarida. I told you this already."

"You did. You struggled a lot. But, believe me, Dona Glória worked far harder than you."

"I'm waiting. What did she do?"

"Took care of me, fed me, and educated me."

"That's it?"

"You don't think that's much? You have no idea what it cost her, the kind of strength it took. Way more than it took for you to get São Bernardo. And I'm positive Dona Glória would never trade me for São Bernardo."

Vanity. The teachers' college churned out little primary school teachers by the dozen. A property like São Bernardo was different.

"There's no comparison."

"We lived in a knife-thrower's house," said Madalena. "There were two chairs. If we had a guest, Dona Glória sat on a kerosene can. The little dining area was my study. The table had a broken leg, so we propped it against the wall. That's where I worked, for years. At night we turned down the oil lamp to save money. Dona Glória would go into the kitchen to mutter, cry, lament. That's how she got into the habit of whispering and walking on tiptoe. The two of us slept in one narrow bed. If I got sick, Dona Glória would sit up all night; when she couldn't stand it anymore, she lay down on the floor."

Madalena fell silent. I was deeply moved by such poverty. "The hell! You really were served a dry dog."

"But Dona Glória never got sick," Madalena continued. "I'd leave for school, and she'd put on her shawl, and go try to make a living. She had so many jobs. She knew priests, so she did flower arranging, alphabetized baptism registries, decorated altars. She knew chief judges, so she made copies of trial proceedings. At night, she sold tickets at the Floriano.

Since our neighbor the baker was illiterate, she kept his accounts in a notebook on the shop counter. Obviously, all these paltry jobs didn't pay too well."

"You have to understand…" I murmured vaguely, looking at the heifers' red backs poking out of the molasses grass.

Madalena interrupted me. "And still, when I had exams, she found time to negotiate with the examiners, God, and the whole world so that I wouldn't fail. Dona Glória is tireless. What she can't do is stick to a steady job; she's left so many unfinished. That's why she's so restless. Here, there aren't any cinema tickets, trial records, baptism registries, baker's account books. Dona Glória sees your machines and your men who work like machines. And yet she's trying to be useful: she goes to the church, she puts flowers on the altars, and cleans the glass on the pictures in the sacristy. She tries to cook, but she and Maria das Dores don't see eye to eye. She offers to help Sr. Ribeiro. She even tried to type."

A truck rolled past in the direction of the sawmill; dull ax thuds issued from the woods; oxcarts creaked along the edge of Bom-Sucesso.

"Like I said, I don't agree with wasting energy that way. People should get in the habit of doing a single thing."

"Dona Glória wouldn't have earned anything if she'd perfected selling cinema tickets or inscribing baptisms: the pay would have always been inadequate."

"Why didn't she get herself hired at some better-paying job?"

"It's hard. But someone's always needed to sell tickets and copy records."

I held my tongue. I didn't feel any sympathy for poor Dona Glória. She was an old backstabber without enough to keep her busy, who wouldn't let go of anything she picked up. Those scattered jobs irritated me. I shrugged but, not wanting to upset Madalena, I said, "You could be right. I disagree. But to each his own."

23

IT WAS Sunday afternoon. I was coming back from the cotton gin and the sawmill, where I'd argued with the machinist. A corroded flywheel and a jammed generator; the man had promised to set everything right in a couple of days. A setback. Heaps of wood; cotton filling the storeroom.

"Shirkers."

I came across old Margarida sitting on a rock by the creek. She was washing her shins, which were scrawny as twigs.

"Good afternoon, Mother Margarida."

"Praise be to Jesus Christ Our Lord," the old lady responded, trying to recognize me with her nose and ears. Between scents and sounds, she made me out. "Oh!"

"How's everything going, Mother Margarida? Are you okay?"

"We get by, my son. Better than I deserve, by God." The old lady dried her skinny legs on her striped linen skirt.

"Is there anything you need over in your hut?"

"I don't need anything! I have everything. The mistress sends everything, a tyranny of luxury: sheets, shoes, so many clothes! What for? Shoes don't fit on my feet. I don't cover myself at night. All I need is a mat. A mat and a fire."

"All right, Mother Margarida. Take care."

I left, vexed at Madalena. Marciano was on the other bank, driving the cattle.

"Wait there."

Going over the plank footbridge, I had a look at the most recent Limousin-Caracu crossbreed.

"Awfully thin." It wasn't, but that's how I was seeing it. "Don't answer—keep your trap shut."

It was Madalena's fault, for giving Rosa a silk dress. Sure, the dress had a tear. But it was a misstep. "You should've thrown it out," I'd said to Madalena. "If it's ripped, throw it out. Don't think about the money—think of the harm it does, giving silk dresses to humble folk."

Madalena's response? She was spitting rivets. We were thunderclouds for a week. Anger chewed me up inside.

The roof of the sawmill was a red smudge tinged black by the rains. Across the creek, Margarida's bent head moved slowly above the grass stems on the bank. Marciano's small figure herded the stock up the footpath.

"Stupid woman!" I exclaimed, furious, thinking of Rosa's dress and old Margarida's sheets. "Squandering!" Then I remembered the flywheel and the generator. "Stupid woman!" Obviously, Madalena had nothing to do with the cotton gin or the sawmill, but that wasn't how I was thinking. Everything got muddled together, so my rage blew up all out of proportion. I forgot the presents that I myself gave Rosa years ago (face powder, bead necklaces) and all the money I'd spent on Margarida, including sending a car into the backlands, including the stereotypes for Gondim's paper. It seemed to me that Madalena was spending for nothing.

"For nothing, get it?" I repeated, convincing myself. "For nothing. Squandering."

Margarida's little white head had already disappeared into the molasses grass. Marciano's shape had vanished around a bend in the road. In the sunset, the roof of the sawmill was even redder.

Maybe I should fire the machinist.

"These people!"

I focused on the problem of the generator, since that was what had gotten me thinking about the shoes, the sheets, the silk dress, the waste! I calmed down. Get rid of the machinist. Yessir, good solution.

Lingering a moment, I watched a couple of seedeaters brazenly making love. Shameless lust. Within two days, they'd go their separate ways, no explanations needed. Lucky.

I headed for the house. On the porch, Madalena, Padilha, Dona Glória, and Sr. Ribeiro were all talking. As soon as I arrived, they fell silent.

I pulled out a chair and sat a little ways from them. Their conversation was likely not all that interesting, but I suspected they were saying bad things about me. Most likely. Dona Glória, always with little secrets for Sr. Ribeiro's ears. And Madalena listening to Padilha. Padilha, who had a low character, in her opinion. Go to hell. All so nice to each other, so amused, so lively. A conspiracy. Or maybe not. But for a guy like me, with a bee in my bonnet? Aggravating.

They looked uneasy, probably trying to puzzle out what I was thinking. Padilha forced his rotten teeth into a fawning smile.

I got up, leaned against the balustrade, and started filling my pipe, turning my back on all the nastiness in my house.

A kid passed through the courtyard, carrying a sling. Goes to show what the school was good for—look at him, loafing, killing birds, taking a day off instead of learning to spell or doing his homework.

Six thousand for charts, maps, and pictures just to pretty up the walls. Six thousand!

Scowling, I watched Madalena out of the corner of my eye. She was as serene as if none of this had anything to do with her.

I furiously lit my pipe. I needed a distraction. Margarida's hut was hidden among the banana trees. Marciano left the stable, staggering and stooped. In front of the manor house, he took off his hat and hid his cigarette. The quarry was almost invisible now since the road leading up to it had grown over.

City hall didn't want any more stones, and our building projects at the ranch were done. Yet every week, Mestre Caetano, moaning in his cot, received a packet of money from Madalena. Yessir: a gravy train. Visitors, medicines from the pharmacy, chickens.

"Nothing like being a cripple."

Sure, he needed it all. But if I supported everyone in need, it'd ruin me.

On top of all this, the silk dresses for Rosa, the shoes and sheets for Margarida. Without consulting me. How was I getting this kind of cheek? It was abuse, thievery—thievery and nothing but.

I went back to my seat. Now Madalena was talking with Padilha, but I couldn't make out what they were saying. They weren't so shy anymore. Padilha had his eyes lowered.

Why hadn't I kicked Padilha out of the house? That parasite, taking me for a hundred and fifty milreis a month for that bogus school and stirring things up, obviously stirring things up.

I turned away and rested my gaze on the bright white courtyard, covered with gravel and sand. At this hour, the place was lousy with pigeons, walking, flying low, strutting around, pecking the ground. I counted some fifty, lost count, started again without getting to the end. There were easily two hundred.

Just a little while ago all this was nothing but spiderweeds and mud. The creek was a dribble of murky water in a narrow, winding gully, spilling onto the plain, drenching the soil, with Mendonça's fences creeping closer and closer.

What a difference! I wanted to jump up and shout, "Have a look around. Are you all asleep? Wake up! Houses, church, roadway, dam, pastures—they're all brand new. The cotton field—almost three miles long and half as wide. The woods—a treasure chest! Every pau d'arco! Every cedar! Look at the cotton gin, the sawmill. You think it all just appeared one day?"

Padilha went on chatting with Madalena. I shrugged.

"To hell with you all! I've had it!"

Sr. Ribeiro kept nodding agreement at Dona Glória's rot.

Casimiro Lopes came and sat on the bottom step. He carved a match with his knife and rolled a straw-paper cigarette, casting his doggy eyes over the meadow, dam, church, crops. Poor Casimiro Lopes. I'd forgotten him. Silent, loyal, ready for anything, he was the only person who understood me. He gave me a sad smile. I stuck out my lip, silently telling him, "It's not going to end well, Casimiro."

Casimiro Lopes flared his nostrils, a grimace of disgust.

The others droned on. For crying out loud! Like bugs. It wasn't worth the bother, taking such drivel seriously. Silly people.

I stood, yawning. I was tired. In the field all day long, checking up on everything, keeping a close eye out. My legs felt feeble. Tired.

Night came. Gloom inside the house. I remembered the jammed generator. Always something. I left the porch and went in. "Maria das Dores, light the lamps."

The baby bellowed like a weaned calf. I couldn't help myself—I marched back and shouted at Dona Glória and Madalena. "Go see to the runt. Is this any way to act? Sitting here jabbering? The world could fall down around you. The kid's bawling."

Madalena had had a little boy.

24

I'D BEEN married for two years, and so João Nogueira, Padre Silvestre, and Azevedo Gondim came for a supper with us.

Now—it was on this very day that I told off Luís Padilha. He forced out some apologies. I didn't pay much heed at the time, but it turned out I should have.

"Say, Padilha, get over here," I'd said to him that morning in the garden, where he was collecting flowers. "This isn't a jail. If you don't like the job, take off."

"What are you talking about, Sr. Paulo?" he exclaimed, stunned.

"Now you want to know what I'm talking about? You're picking flowers! Look at the clock, man."

"It was Dona Madalena. She sent me to pick roses."

"What are you, a gardener? Dona Madalena doesn't give the orders. Stop going around yapping and wasting my time."

"It's not my fault," Padilha defended himself. "Take it up with her. The young lady asked me for flowers to decorate the table for this afternoon. What am I supposed to do? Turn her down? And as for conversation, Sr. Paulo, sir, you have to understand: she's an educated woman set down in the sticks! She needs someone she can count on once in a while for agreeable and varied exchanges."

I thought this was pretty funny and put Padilha out of

my mind. He hastily tore up a rosebush, pricking his fingers on the thorns, and stole away. Agreeable exchanges!

Later on, though, in the study, a vague idea leapt into my head, messed around for an instant, and slipped away. When I tried to grasp it, it shrank away even further. I stopped reading the letter in front of me and, without knowing why, looked at Madalena suspiciously. She was leaning against the writing desk, standing and riffling the pages of the ledger, and looking through the window at the pau d'arco trees in the distance.

I signed the paper mechanically; mechanically, Madalena handed me another. All at once, the idea returned, though it moved so fast I barely registered it. I trembled. Madalena's face appeared to have changed. But the impression was fleeting.

I buried myself in work and, in the afternoon, when our friends climbed out of the automobile, I was perfectly calm. "Well, now, nice to see you all."

They don't stand on ceremony. We went inside and quenched Gondim's thirst. Any time he comes to São Bernardo, he needs brandy.

Everyone was very lively during supper. Even I joined the fray, despite my total ignorance of the subjects under debate.

To start with, Azevedo Gondim, tongue loosened by the brandy, praised country living. "This is the life! I'd like to see anyone raise a turkey of this size, scratching around in a backyard in the city. What a plump beast! God bless it."

Dona Glória tut-tutted and shifted her eyes away from the center of the table, where a turkey squatted on a platter, receiving all this extravagant praise.

Following her, Padre Silvestre cast his eyes over the flower beds and the groves. "It really must be delightful to live in this paradise. Such beauty!"

"For outsiders," I broke in. "We're used to it here. In the final analysis, I'm not cultivating all this for decoration. It's to sell."

"Even the flowers?" asked Azevedo Gondim.

"Everything. Flowers, vegetables, fruit . . ."

"That's exactly right!" Padre Silvestre exclaimed, nodding his grizzled head and furrowing his narrow brow. "That's the way! If all Brazilians thought like that, we wouldn't be going through such hard times."

"Politics, Padre Silvestre?" João Nogueira questioned, smiling.

Padre Silvestre glared with his dim little eyes. "Why not? You have to admit, sir, that we are on the verge of an abyss."

Padre Silvestre is all mixed up. He's got a hardworking parish, but his head's in the clouds. Liberal as hell.

Padilha stuck his nose into the exchange. "Hear, hear."

"An abyss," Padre Silvestre repeated.

"What abyss?" Azevedo Gondim asked.

The reverend worked up a forceful response. "What we see all around us. The bankruptcy of the regime. Dishonesty, villainy."

"Who're the villains?" inquired João Nogueira.

Padre Silvestre stuck out his lower lip and got evasive. His opinions are the newspapers' opinions, but since those are contradictory and he can't handle disagreement, he only reads the opposition's papers. He believes them, apart from his occasional experiments with doubt. The papers swear that government men are scoundrels, but the fact that he knows a few respectable ones weakened his faith in the printed word. In the end, to make his thinking consistent with what he read, he decided that individual politicians might be like anyone but collectively they're thugs. "Come on! It's not my place to denounce anyone. Facts are facts. Use your eyes."

"It's good to name names," João Nogueira insisted.

"For what? The dominant faction is crumbling into dust. The country's on the rocks, good sir. That's what I say: the country's on the rocks."

I passed him a bottle and inquired, "What happened to you that you got these ideas, sir? You in trouble? From what little I know, people only talk like this when income isn't covering expenses. I sure hope your affairs are in decent shape."

"Don't talk about me. It's the state's finances that are in bad shape. Finances and everything else. But don't fool yourselves. There has to be a revolution!"

"That's just what we need. To smash this seesaw."

"Why?" asked Madalena.

"You a revolutionary too?" I exclaimed rudely.

"I'm only asking why."

"Why! Because no one can get credit anymore, the exchange rate is dropping, the foreign market is on the brink of death. Not to speak of the political jumble."

"It would be magnificent," Madalena interrupted. "Afterward, everything would straighten out."

"Absolutely," concurred Luís Padilha.

"Do you all know what you're saying?"

"What baffles me is that Padre Silvestre wants revolution," said Nogueira. "How would he benefit?"

"I wouldn't," responded the vicar. "Not at all. But our society would benefit greatly."

"You're all waiting for that," Azevedo Gondim broke in. "You're making a bonfire, sirs, and you're going to roast in it."

"Fables!" muttered Padilha.

"It's not a fable!" shouted Azevedo Gondim. "If a fight breaks out, something interesting's going to come out of it—right, Nogueira?"

"Fascism."

"That's what you all want. What we'll get is communism."

Dona Glória crossed herself and Sr. Ribeiro opined, "God save us."

"Are you afraid, Sr. Ribeiro?" Madalena asked, smiling.

"I've seen many transformations already, excellent lady, all bad."

"It wouldn't be anything like that," Padre Silvestre stated. "We wouldn't adopt alien doctrines here. Communism is disaster—societal unrest, hunger."

Sr. Ribeiro passed his fingers over his shiny bald spot. "In the time of Dom Pedro, little money circulated. Anyone who had a conto of réis was rich. But there was plenty— pumpkins rotted on the vine. Castor beans, cottonseeds, all free for the taking. With the proclamation of the republic, they became worth their weight in gold. For this reason, I say change brings nothing but trouble. The railroad—"

"A country without God!" cried Padre Silvestre to Dona Glória. "They shot all the priests. Not a single one escaped. And the soldiers, drunk, desecrated the saints and danced on the altars."

Dona Glória whimpered, hands on her bosom. "How horrible! Could it be? On the altars!"

"They didn't desecrate anything," Padilha interposed. "That's counterrevolutionary propaganda."

"That's what you're rooting for, Padre Silvestre," exclaimed Gondim.

The vicar absolved himself. "Not me. I'm keeping to myself. Now, do I think the government is bad? Sure, I think so. Is there an urgent need for reforms? Yes, there is. As for communism, that's a lie. It won't catch on. Rest easy—between us, it won't catch on. Our people have religion. Our people are Catholic."

João Nogueira disagreed. "That's exactly what they're not. No one knows doctrine. Any Protestant singing hymns and evangelizing has a parade of devotees trailing after him. Then there's the spiritualists, and the rabble with their fetishism and tree worship. Lots of people think of Catholicism as though it's a restaurant. They choose a dish without any particular appetite and then put down their knife and fork. The ones who get the furthest get indigestion. You're fooling yourself, Padre Silvestre: these people attend mass, but they're not Catholic, and it's as easy to get them to lean one way as another."

Padre Silvestre was thrown off. "In that case . . ."

But João Nogueira had finished. He was chatting with me, in a low voice, deriding Sr. Magalhães.

Madalena was speaking with Sr. Ribeiro. "What do you stand to lose, sir?"

"I don't know, excellent lady. Maybe I would lose, since all that ever comes my way is misfortune. I finally have a bit of bread here. But if such an unfortunate thing came to pass, it wouldn't bring me anything."

Madalena tried to convince him, but I couldn't tell what she was saying. All of a sudden, I was invaded by suspicion. I'd experienced a similar, disagreeable feeling before. When?

João Nogueira was annihilating Sr. Magalhães. Dona

Glória, overcome by food and heat, was closing her eyes, already indifferent to the foretold danger. Bullheaded Sr. Ribeiro wanted no innovations. And Azevedo Gondim, red-faced, was testifying to Padre Silvestre: "There aren't. Nogueira is right, there aren't. I know men who defend religion in the newspapers and never look at a Bible."

When? Everything became clear in an instant: it had been that same day in the study, when Madalena was bringing me letters to sign.

Yessir! She was colluding with Padilha, trying to get my trustworthy employees to stray from the path. Yessir, a communist! I was building up and she was tearing down.

We all got up and went into the living room to have coffee.

"Yessir, a communist!"

"It's corruption, the dissolution of the family," Padre Silvestre persisted.

No one responded.

I myself am ignorant about these things, of course, but I wanted to hear what Madalena thought of them. All the vicar did was shout. What would Madalena's opinion be?

"On this point, Padre Silvestre is right," Gondim agreed. "Religion is a bridle."

"Bunkum!" said Nogueira. "Are we horses who need bridles?"

What could religion mean to Madalena? Maybe nothing. I'd never brought it up with her.

"Monstrous." I repeated it, in a low voice, slowly and without conviction. "Monstrous."

A materialist. I remember hearing Costa Brito speaking about historical materialism. What did historical materialism mean?

The truth is that I don't worry about the next world. I believe in God, the heavenly paymaster of my workers, so poorly compensated here on earth, and I believe in the devil, who'd someday torture the thief that stole one of my pedigreed cows. In other words, I don't have much religion, although that's partly because it doesn't matter much for a man. But a woman without religion is an abomination.

Communist, materialist. Some marriage! Friendship with Padilha, that imbecile. "Pleasant and varied exchanges." What were those exchanges about? Social reforms, or worse things. I had no idea! A woman without religion is capable of anything.

"No doubt," I responded to some balderdash Padre Silvestre slung at me.

Sr. Ribeiro and Azevedo Gondim were listlessly badgering each other. Dona Glória was snoozing. Padilha smoked in a corner.

"Probably."

I must have been talking rubbish, because Padre Silvestre disagreed and beat me over the head with some proof I couldn't understand.

I looked for Madalena and saw her engrossed with Nogueira, smiling, in the window nook.

I'm a confident man. But I was struck by Nogueira's fine eyes, his well-made clothes, his smooth voice. I thought about my eighty-nine kilos, this red face with its thick brows. Disgruntled, I crossed my enormous, hairy hands, rough from long years of farming. I mixed all this with Madalena's materialism and communism . . . and I got jealous.

25

I GOT JEALOUS. At first I wanted to grab Padilha by the ears and boot him out. But I kept him on to get my revenge. I expelled him from the house, which is to say I imprisoned him in the school. He lived there—slept and ate there, cold grub on a tray.

I let four months go by without paying his salary. And when I saw him defeated, thin, with a dirty collar and long hair, I taunted him. "Have patience. You'll get even soon enough. You're a prophet. Keep writing your little stories about the proletariat."

The wretch defended himself. But the humiliation went on and, in the end, he was forced to swallow all of it. One day, he came crying, sobbing, begging me to arrange a post for him in the State Treasury.

"Impossible, Padilha. Wait for the Soviets. You'll get a post easily in the Red Guard, and when it happens, Padilha, old buddy, you won't give me a second thought."

In the manor house, guarded by Shark and Casimiro Lopes, life was a sorrow, an aggravation. Dona Glória passed her afternoons under the orange trees, stuffing herself on brochures and leaflets. Madalena embroidered, her face covered in shadows.

At times, the shadows brightened. Toward the end of the

workday, our surroundings encouraged lazy conversation, snoozing, sloth.

A breeze would blow, bringing me shivers of pleasure, making me want to stretch. I'd look toward the peak and the red ribbon of road winding around it, the woods, the cotton fields, the still water of the dam.

Madalena would put aside her embroidery and pierce the landscape with her eyes. Her eyes would grow wide. Beautiful eyes.

Without even stirring, we would feel ourselves growing closer, cautiously, each afraid of hurting the other. Cautious smiles and vague gestures.

I'd talk about the backlands. Madalena would recall tidbits about teachers' college. That dampened the mood, without fail. Teachers' college! Silveira used to talk about vocational students painting the town red. He knows public institutions like the back of his hand, even wrote regulations. Girls learn a lot at teachers' college.

I don't like clever women. The ones calling themselves intellectuals are abominations. Some recite verses in theaters— I've seen them giving lectures, dragging around a husband or something close enough. They speak prettily enough on the stage, but in private, behind closed doors, they say, "Come look after me, my dear."

They've never said that to me, but they have to Nogueira. Just think. They appear in the cities of the backland, smiling, selling pamphlets, giving lectures, etc. They've probably infested the state capitals. Abominations.

Madalena wasn't an intellectual, properly speaking. But she didn't care about religion and she read the foreign news.

I shrank back, morose.

Flirting with Nogueira, in front of the window, smiling!

Smiling exactly like the others, the ones that give lectures. Danger: anyone who messes with João Nogueira comes to grief. A good lawyer, straight in his dealings—*yes, yes, no, no*—but when it comes to women, he's a trap. A fox in a henhouse. Was this conversation even the first? They knew each other before I stumbled in headlong. Maybe they even kept company. When I met Madalena at Judge Magalhães's house, João Nogueira had been there. Dull, that Magalhães, incredibly dull. Listening to him is worse than listening to a saw go through wood. "I'm a judge, understand? A judge. I get up in the morning." Nogueira, with his keen eye, putting up with that? Interesting. When he had started talking politics, Madalena had lifted her head, curious. Now, after two years of marriage, she was falling all over him in the window nook.

I drew myself up and insulted her mentally: "Slut!"

With Padilha, even! How the hell does she have the guts to approach a leper like Padilha? On the social problem.

"The hell with the social problem. This here is shamelessness."

Then there were the contributions to Gondim's paper. She was still contributing. Not much, but still. She and Gondim had been hand in glove. Remember that afternoon that he had stupidly congratulated me? Familiarity. And they used to discuss her legs and her breasts!

What was I thinking, trusting such a woman? An intellectual woman.

My expression must have been terrible, because Madalena blanched, practically trembling.

If I knew...knew what? Does any husband ever know anything?

The mestizos working my fields might be mocking me.

Even Marciano and Rosa could be making comments on it, in bed at night.

Did Marciano know about my relations with Rosa? I doubt it. I was always careful to send him off shopping in the city, a good excuse. And maybe he didn't want to know. Let's face it, he wasn't the sharpest knife in the drawer.

"Ultimately, no one can be sure, truly sure."

What would Sr. Ribeiro say? What would Dona Glória say?

I left, slowly, to go look at the little boy, crawling between rooms, falling over, abandoned. I picked him up and examined him. He was thin. He had blond hair, like his mother's. Light eyes. Mine are dark. A snub nose. Children usually have snub noses.

I couldn't decide, and quit looking so closely. He didn't have my features, but it's not as though he had any other man's.

The little boy kept on dragging himself around, falling, crying, ugly as sin. His little arms and legs were painfully thin. He screamed day and night, screamed like a condemned man, the nanny going crazy for lack of sleep. There'd been times he bellowed so hard he turned purple. I was scared he'd die when Padre Silvestre wet his head in the font. When he started teething, he broke out in boils. They covered him with bandages, like a crossbred calf. No one cared about him. Dona Glória read. Madalena went here and there, sighing, her eyelids red. "She doesn't even love her own child!" I thought to myself.

The baby cried, cried nonstop. Casimiro Lopes was the one person who was friendly to him. He'd carry him out to the porch and sit parroting words back and forth with him, tell him stories of jaguars, sing him to sleep with songs of the backlands. The little boy would rise up onto his feet, pulling on Casimiro's beard as he sang,

> "I was born at seven months
> And raised without a mother's breast
> I drank the milk of a hundred cows
> At the gate of the corral."

Good soul, Casimiro Lopes. I never saw anyone less complicated. I'm convinced he has no memory of the evil he's done. Everyone thinks he's wild, but that's overdoing it. He only goes wild occasionally. He understands nothing, can barely express himself, and is innocent as a savage.

26

I WAS GOING from bad to worse. I looked sick, sick as can be, even to myself. Loathing, constant anxiety, rage. Madalena, Padilha, Dona Glória—what a trio! I wanted to take Madalena and slap her to high heaven, right across the mouth, and slap Dona Glória, too, who spent years working like a dray horse to raise that little snake.

Insignificant facts swelled all out of proportion. One gesture, one meaningless word raised my suspicion.

Teachers' college women! Silveira had forewarned me, or hinted, at least. Now I had to put up with the consequences of my mistake, or be made a fool of.

Putting up with it! Putting up with it after all this! With this disgrace? Why should I? I needed proof: to catch her unawares in the bedroom, in bed with someone else.

The idea of catching her obsessed me. I rummaged in her bags and books; I opened her correspondence. Madalena cried, screamed, had an attack of nerves, then more attacks, then more crying, more screaming, one outburst after another. It was a living hell.

One day, passing by the ranch, Judge Magalhães came in for lunch. Watching him closely, I could tell he was laying it on thick with Madalena. He wasn't actually saying anything wrong, as far as I knew, but the way he acted, looked, and smiled said more than enough. There were ambiguous whispers and gestures, or so it appeared to me.

That night I couldn't get to sleep. I sat up for hours, hating Madalena, who was curled up in a corner of the bed, legs tucked against her stomach.

With Magalhães, an old man! But then I was an old man myself, I reflected, and scratched my beard sadly. I was partly to blame—I didn't look after myself. Busy as hell with the farm, I would go days without shaving. When I returned from doing chores, I'd be caked in mud up to my eyeballs like a pig. I'd take a hot bath, but no kind of scrubbing can get rid of all that.

What huge hands! My palms were massive, chapped, calloused, hard as a horse's hoof. Huge fingers too, short and thick. What was I doing, caressing a female with hands like these!

Magalhães made a living off his pen—he had hands soft as kid leather. His manicured nails certainly wouldn't scratch. All he ever hoisted was documents!

Madalena breathed deeply, sound asleep. So slender, so delicate. She'd been getting thin.

I got up and moved into the light. My hands really were huge. I went over to the mirror. Magalhães was pretty ugly, but me—living this life of a thousand devils, bellowing at mestizos all day in the sun—I was dreadful. Burnt. Those eyebrows! My hair was grizzled, but my beard was nearly white. Unshaven! What a filthy bum!

The next day, I found Madalena writing. I crept over on tiptoe and read Azevedo Gondim's address.

"Do me a favor and let me see that?"

Madalena grabbed a page she hadn't folded yet. "You don't have to see it. It's only of interest to me."

"Sure. But it'd be a good idea for you to let me see it. Do me the favor?"

"Didn't I just say it has nothing to do with you? What a nuisance!"

"Show me the letter," I insisted, taking her by the shoulders.

Madalena defended it, holding the paper away in her outstretched hand, hiding it behind her back. "Go to hell, mind your own business."

This resistance enraged me. "Show me the letter, slut."

Madalena pulled free and ran toward the bedroom, screaming, "Cur!"

Dona Glória came to the door, shocked. "For the love of God! They can hear outside."

I lost my head. "Go to fucking hell! Are you deaf, standing there with your little angel face? That's right: fucking hell. And if you think that's bad, there's the street. You and your fine niece, understand? Go to fucking hell, both of you!"

Dona Glória fled with her handkerchief over her eyes.

"Thug!" Madalena cried.

All I could say was, "Show me the letter, slut."

Madalena tore the paper into bits and threw them out the window. "Thug!" She left in a whirlwind. In the hall, she screamed, "Murderer!"

Stunned, I murmured, "Bitch." I stood still and watched the bits of paper fly across the garden in the morning wind, between the leaves of the rosebushes. Far away, in the living room or kitchen, Madalena continued screaming, "Murderer!"

The other ugly names she'd called me meant nothing. Not this one. That's what bothered me. Women are sensitive creatures. They shouldn't get themselves mixed up in men's business.

Before her, the only person who'd branded me a murderer face to face was Costa Brito, in the free section of the *Gazeta*. Just when I'd given him what he deserved, I'd gotten yoked to Madalena. Damned yoke! I'd have been better off with a broken leg, right? A friendly arrangement is worth more than some marriages.

Murderer! That was unexpected. How'd she come up with that? By accident? Or had she read Brito's newspaper? Most likely, Padilha alluded to the rumors. Yessir! Padilha. What evil wasn't he capable of? Funny. Padilha!

A memory, Jaqueira's house, appeared and disappeared almost as quick. Instead, my mind started repeating, "Murderer! Murderer!" How stupid was I, wasting time with this rot? "Madalena, Dona Glória, Padilha, they should go to fucking hell, all of them."

Here I was, making myself crazy, with the ranch hands taking it free and easy. I stretched. I hadn't slept all night! Trembling, I looked at my hands. My hands really looked huge.

Ah, yes: Jaqueira . . . It'd been years.

Madalena—so ungrateful to poor Casimiro Lopes, I suddenly realized. After all . . .

Murderer! What could she know of my life? I had never confided in her. Everyone has secrets. Wouldn't that be interesting—if we all went around telling them to each other. Everyone's got vices. Madalena went to teachers' college—she must have her share. What could I know of her past? The present was bad, though, obviously bad.

And ungrateful on top of it all. Casimiro Lopes took her son out on the porch, rocked him, sang to him, soothed him to sleep. What a mess! What a tumult! She hadn't called Casimiro Lopes a murderer, but me. In that moment, though,

I didn't see anything disjointed about my thoughts. I wouldn't even have batted an eye at someone swearing that Casimiro Lopes and I were one and the same.

Padilha! Bad help has brought down many a man. Who would have supposed that Jaqueira...

Jaqueira's come back. Here, in brief, was the Jaqueira case: Jaqueira was this pasty guy. Punks, pimps with nothing to their names, would beat him up. Jaqueira would take it all and mutter, "I'll kill one of these bastards someday, you'll see."

Everyone slept with his wife. All you had to do was knock. If the wife didn't open the door right away, Jaqueira would open it himself, yawning and threatening, "I'll kill one of these bastards someday, you'll see."

He did. Hid himself behind a beam and fired a shotgun into a customer's heart. The jury condemned him with six (corrupt) votes. Jaqueira got out of jail and became a respected citizen. No one ever meddled with him again.

27

WHEN I calmed down, it seemed to me that I'd gotten myself tied up in knots for nothing. Judge Magalhães was the type to fawn innocently over any lady. And the paper addressed to Gondim must have been an article. What else could it be? Such petty matters, but they'd resulted in a stupid dogfight, crude insults. Maria das Dores heard it. Sr. Ribeiro heard it. For crying out loud!

Madalena was obviously honest. She didn't show me the paper because she wasn't going to let me twist her arm, out of sheer dignity, that was more than clear. Jealous idiot.

You'd have to search a convent to find someone better-behaved than her—discreet, a straight shooter, and caring to a fault, even toward the smallest woodland animals. As for her thoughts, nothing was certain—no one can enter someone else's thoughts—but her words and actions were unimpeachable. She could have called me worse names. Worse than murderer? Okay, that'd be tough. But I'm not complaining about her. I'm complaining about that insolent Padilha.

The morning's violence over, I felt optimistic again, and all my malice turned toward the schoolmaster.

Ingrate! There was nothing to do but fire him. I'd take care of it that same afternoon.

Padilha offered me his chair and took a stool, looking like

a roast chicken. "At your service, Sr. Paulo Honório," he said, seriously.

"Bad news: I no longer need your services."

"Why?" Padilha said, baffled. "What did I do?"

"Come on! Why ask me? You know perfectly well what you did."

"I didn't do anything. What could I have done, locked up here? I have less freedom than prisoners in jail. I don't go out. If I walk twenty paces, it's with Casimiro in the waistband of my trousers. What did I do? Tell me one thing I did."

"I don't explain."

Padilha hung his head. "That's fine. Toe the line, and in the end, this is what you get. Year in, year out, doing more than your share, straight as a fuse, shouldering your responsibilities, trying to please. And just when you expect a raise, you get the boot." He got up. "At least give me a few days to organize my things and chase down another job. I can't just walk out like this, with barely the clothes on my back."

I also got up. "You've got a month to get out."

"Thanks so very much," Padilha stammered. "We're supposed to be grateful, right? That's perfect. If I hadn't been your wife's lackey, none of this would have happened." He got indignant. "A lackey! 'Go get a book, Sr. Padilha.' I would go. 'Bring me some paper, Sr. Padilha.' I would bring it. 'Copy this page, Sr. Padilha.' I copied it. 'Pick some oranges, Sr. Padilha.' Picking oranges? A lackey! That woman brought me down."

"Watch your tongue," I ordered.

"What did I say? That I was a lackey? I was, sir. That's what you're dismissing me for."

"As if! What happened was that you were going around

intriguing, man. Going around scheming, man. Going around plotting, man."

Luís Padilha was dumbfounded. Then, in one breath, he said, "What intrigues, schemes, plots? You haven't shown me a single one, sir. Is it my fault your wife has advanced ideas? If that's what—"

"No, it's not that."

"Then I haven't a clue."

"Listen, Padilha. I'm nearly fifty years old and I've seen a thing or two. I'm not going to mince words. I've spotted lots of things and turned the other cheek, God knows. If I say you're plotting, it's because you're plotting."

Padilha nitpicked. "Tell me what I've done, then. My conscience is clear. Tell me. When people know something, they say it."

"Like a newborn lamb, that's you," I replied, mocking him. "You didn't make up whoppers to tell Madalena? You didn't talk about me? Did you or didn't you?"

"I didn't. Never, Sr. Paulo. I don't know a thing!"

"Time to bring your horse in out of the rain, buddy. I heard."

Padilha was rattled. "Fine. If you heard, we won't argue. Of course, you heard what I never said."

"I heard what you said, all right. Don't deny it. I heard it perfectly well."

"If you heard anything," Padilha conceded, "it was the story of Mendonça's death. Dona Madalena already knew—"

"What did she know?"

"What people say. Slander. I explained everything and defended you, sir. 'Dona Madalena, this is an old case, and getting mixed up in it won't bring anyone back to life. Old Mendonça was an abscess, stealing his neighbors' land. As for what gets spread around, don't believe it: nothing but smears. Sr. Paulo has a good heart and wouldn't harm a fly.'"

I recalled that morning's fight. Exactly what I thought: this bum's rumors. "Say, Padilha, why'd you say Madalena brought you down?"

"Are you denying it, sir? If it weren't for her, I wouldn't have lost my job. It was her. As you can see, I'm not in favor. Many times, I declared, with all my heart, 'Dona Madalena, Sr. Paulo detests socialism. You'd better drop these games, ma'am. These conversations are not helping.' Like that. The parrot eats the corn, the parakeet gets the blame. I'm the parakeet."

I felt weak. "What the hell were you two talking about?" My jealousy had become public.

Padilha gave me a phony smile and responded, "Literature, politics, arts, religion. She's an intelligent lady, Dona Madalena. And educated—she's a library. But I'm just raining where it's wet. You know far better than I what kind of wife you've got."

28

"You know what kind of wife you've got."

What a thing to say!

Padilha had to know something. Did he? Or was he just running on at the mouth?

Speculation. I wanted to be sure and have it over and done with. Yes or no.

"You know what kind of wife you've got." I didn't know a thing! This was what had made me lose all appetite. Living with someone under the same roof, eating at the same table, sleeping in the same bed, and realizing, at the end of all those years, she's a stranger! My God! But what if I'm ignorant of what's inside me, if I'm forgetting many of my own actions, and don't even know what I was actually feeling in those months of torture?

You see how we waste time on useless agonizing? Wouldn't it be so much better to be like oxen? Oxen with intelligence. Is there anything stupider than tormenting a living creature for fun? Was I right or wasn't I? What's it all for? Looking for trouble! Was I right or not?

If I'd had some proof that Madalena was innocent, I'd have given her a life like she'd never imagined. I would have bought her countless dresses, expensive hats, silk stockings by the dozen. I would have lavished attention on her, brought the best doctors down from the capital to cure her anemia and help her gain weight. I never would have minded her giving clothes to the workers' wives.

And if I knew that she'd betrayed me? Ah! If I knew she'd betrayed me, I would have killed her, opened a vein in her throat, slowly, so that the blood ran all day.

My own depraved thoughts sickened me. A pointless crime—what good was that that? Better to abandon her, see her suffer. And when she'd been in and out of hospitals, when she was in rags out on the street, starving, all sharp bones, old scars, and fresh wounds, I'd throw her a few coins—for the love of God.

Was I right or not?

It makes no difference. Just when we're most tired, here comes death: the devil carries us off, friends flap their muzzles at the funeral and then forget even the slop they freeloaded.

What was it to me whatever Padilha, Sr. Ribeiro, Dona Glória, Marciano believed? Casimiro Lopes had no beliefs. What I wouldn't give to be like Casimiro Lopes!

"It's going to end badly, Casimiro," I said with my eyes.

Shrugging, Casimiro Lopes agreed.

29

My misgivings got unbearable. I had to confirm them. Madalena had some secret vice, no doubt about it.

"No doubt about it, no doubt, understand? No doubt."

Repeating it over and over made me feel more certain.

I rubbed my hands. No doubt about it. Far better this than flip-flopping from one side to another.

It was obvious that Dona Glória was a procuress. A light tread, lowered eyes, a faint voice—exactly the formula for a procuress. Earlier on, she must have been up the creek. A procuress leading her niece off the path. Always in agreement, those two whores.

Ultimately, Padilha had done me a good turn.

I ranted to myself, enraged. "Thank you, Padilha." Yessir, a fine whore. Every cat and dog in São Bernardo knew what she got up to. "That woman brought me down." How disrespectful! Who would blast a charge like that, straight in her husband's face, about a married woman? Who? No one. Do I make myself clear?

Padre Silvestre came by São Bernardo, and I kept my ear to the ground, suspicious. I was suspicious, God forgive me. Even a tethered horse eats.

My suspicions made another terrifying leap. I realized that Madalena was carrying on with the mestizo farmworkers. The mestizos, yessir.

At times, good sense pulled me up by the ear. "Cool it, bonehead. This doesn't have legs."

Think about it: A properly washed, properly dressed, properly starched, properly educated white woman is not about to snuggle with dark, dirty brutes reeking of sweat. I couldn't trust my own eyes. But if I couldn't trust my own eyes, what could I trust? I saw a field worker winking at her!

I curbed my thoughts, forcing myself to consider other possibilities. Obviously, the wink couldn't be for her. It couldn't be!

Couldn't it? "A woman would sleep with ticks if she could tell which ones were male."

One afternoon, for a whole hour, I watched old Margarida wobble weakly up the hill to visit us, terrified the poor thing was carrying some letter.

Seems to me I was half crazy.

30

THAT NIGHT I thought I heard footsteps in the garden. Why the hell wasn't Shark barking? That good-for-nothing dog was losing his sense of smell.

I got up, grabbed my rifle, blew out the light, opened the window. "Who's there?"

Could it be an enemy—the Gamas' people, Pereira's, Fidélis's? Not likely. The threats had stopped and Casimiro Lopes and I had grown rusty. Instinctively, I flattened against the wall. I thought I made out a figure.

"Who's there? Beast or ghost? Not going to answer?"

In the silence a shot rang out. The neighbors were alarmed. Madalena jumped out of bed, screaming.

"What happened?" she whimpered, terrified.

"It's your accomplices, circling the house. But don't kid yourself: someday you'll find one of those bastards shot out there."

Madalena lay among the pillows, arms wrapped around herself, sobbing.

Someone whistled in the distance—a signal?

"Did you hear that whistle? What did you do, set up a meeting here in the bedroom, right on top of me? That's all I need. You want me to leave? If you want me to leave, just say so. Don't be shy."

Madalena cried like a fountain.

I grew sad. A brute, a monstrous brute.

What if the footfalls and the whistle weren't about her? Ah! If that were the case, a spear through the tongue would be letting me off easy. What if the footfalls and the whistle hadn't even happened? I recalled one night: I was going out of my mind and pulled out my double-edged knife—on a rat, as it turned out. Mistakes happen all the time.

I backed off. "Cut the boo-hooing. You don't have to fall apart just because someone's whistling in the orchard and walking in the garden. Enough with the show."

Madalena cried and cried, until, tears exhausted, she fell asleep. I curled up on the edge of the bed so as not to touch her. Just as I was nodding off, I caught the creak of a key in the lock and the noise of someone lifting the roof tiles. I woke with a start and held my breath. Who was poking at the doors? Who'd be pulling the tiles off the roof?

I edged over to Madalena and took a look at her face. Had she heard? Was she pretending to sleep?

I got up, dragged a chair over, sat down. Madalena stayed asleep.

No one would fiddle with the lock or tiles. I'd dreamed it. Did I also make up the steps? A nightmare. That had to be it. A nightmare. Even the whistle might've been an owl's screech.

The clock in the dining room struck once. What time was it? Half past? One? Half past one? Or halfway through some other hour?

I couldn't sleep. I counted from one to one hundred, and folded my pinky finger. I counted from one hundred to two hundred, folded its neighbor, and so forth, up to a thousand, two fists. I counted to a hundred again and released my thumb; another hundred, trigger finger; at two thousand, my two hands were open. I repeated this foolishness, imagining that for each finger I moved a conto of réis profit into the balance column, so much money I got sick of it and stopped counting.

The clock struck again. One o'clock? Half past one? Just go see. I got up, with heavy steps. Madalena continued to sleep.

I unlocked and locked the door to the hallway. I unlocked it again and locked it again. I peered at Madalena's face. Such a deep sleep! She lay there as though everything was fine, while I was chewed up inside. I wanted to shake her awake, get back to the battle that had become our lives. Sleeping like that, while I was tormented, tortured? So unfair. Tormented by what—in the end, what was I doing here, my hand on the key and my eyes bulging at Madalena?

"Why the hell am I up and about?"

Ah, right: to check the time. I pushed open the door, went down the hall, entered the dining room. Always good to know what time it is.

I sat at my place at the table. When our fights began, I'd sit here every night, arguing with Madalena. We'd wasted so many words!

"Why do people argue, defending themselves? What for?"

What for, really? What I wanted to say was simple and direct, though it was useless to hope my wife would ever be clear or concise. Her vast, slippery vocabulary was a closed room to me, and when she tried to use my rough, basic language, the mildest, most solid expressions sounded snakelike: twisting, biting, venomous.

31

ONE AFTERNOON I climbed the church tower to watch Marciano hunt owls. Some had nested in the roof, and at night the screeches split our ears. I wanted those cursed birds gone for good.

Up top, I listened to Marciano's racket, though I couldn't see him, while through four little windows open to the four corners of the sky, I contemplated the landscape. Through one of them, I saw a bit of my study, below—a desk and my wife seated at the desk, writing. Moving on from this familiar, commonplace scene, I made out the side of the house—doors, windows, Dona Glória's bed, a corner of the dining room. I lifted my head to the horizon: tiles, plaster, and roof ornaments. Above those: fields, mountains, clouds.

The molasses grass was cropped low, with oxen grazing there, looking like plastic toys. The cotton fields climbed uphill and downhill, to appear again, faded, in the distance. In the dark shadows of a clearing in the woods, nearly black, the cotton pickers' tiny figures were faintly visible.

An owl hooted. Marciano crawled out of his hiding place, woolly hair white with spiderwebs. "I got another, Sr. Paulo, a whopper of an owl."

I grumbled to myself, "What's that stubborn bitch thinking? Writing. How stupid!"

Marciano's Rosa crossed the creek. She lifted her skirts to her waist, dropping them once she got past the deepest part. When she reached the bank, she stood still for an instant, her legs apart, dripping water, then shimmied off, her rear bouncing seductively.

The hilltops were rounded by the distance and gilded by the sun. They looked otherworldly, like saints' heads.

"If that nitwit paid attention, if she had even an iota of sense, she'd be up here taking in this cornucopia of beauty."

Feeling content, I came down the stairs as dusk fell. Although I'm only a somewhat sensitive person, I was convinced that the world wasn't that bad. To stand fifty feet above the earth feels like growing fifty feet. When you're gigantic like that, looking down at all the herds below, vast lands stretching out, planted fields, all yours; when you see the smoke rising from your houses, where folks live who fear, respect, maybe even love you, because they depend on you—a massive serenity enfolds you. You feel good. You feel strong. If your enemies are dying off, even enemies so weak that any punk could smash them with a club, you feel yourself getting even stronger. In the face of all this, a doll tracing invisible lines on a nearly invisible sheet of paper is almost beneath thought. So I came down the stairs at peace with God and men, hoping I might finally get some relief from those damned screeches.

Mulling all this over, I crossed the garden toward the orchard, anxious to see if the pruning was going as it should.

By the study, I found a piece of writing paper on the ground, likely blown there by the wind. I unfolded it and looked indifferently at Madalena's pretty, round handwriting. To be honest, I couldn't understand what it said. Some words I didn't know, others I might have recognized if they weren't used in such a confusing way that I had no way to grasp them. It was probably well written—my wife knew grammar up, down, and sideways—but it was covered in scratch marks and insertions, perfectly fine sentences crossed out. Even if it wasn't of any use, I tried to justify the corrections: "Using trickery to disguise what should be plain!"

I walked among the orange trees, the pruning forgotten. I reread the page and sorted through hazy ideas shuffled together in my mind. I shuddered. Dammit! It was a section of a letter, a letter to a man. There was no addressee—the beginning was missing—but it was a letter to a man, no doubt about it.

I read the page a third time, dazed, lingering over clear expressions and trying to decipher obscure ones.

"Here's the proof," I muttered, astonished. "Who's this filth for?"

My suspicions fell first on João Nogueira, Sr. Magalhães, Azevedo Gondim, and Silveira of the teachers' college. I reread the letter over and over, swearing like a condemned man, my temples pounding.

Finally, night fell. I couldn't make the words out any longer.

Yessir! A letter to a man.

For a long time, I walked under the fruit trees. "Am I some son-of-a-bitch Marciano?"

I returned furious, ready to be over and done with this misery. My ears were buzzing. Red stripes danced in front of my eyes.

Blinded, I ran straight into Madalena, who was leaving the church.

"About-face," I commanded, grabbing hold of her arm. "We have business."

"Again?" Madalena asked. She let me lead her into the darkness of the church.

I lit a candle and leaned against the table filled with saints, on the platform where Padre Silvestre wore his liturgical garments on mass days. "What were you doing here? Praying? You're not above claiming to pray."

"Again?" Madalena repeated.

I half hoped she'd hurl insults, but I was mistaken: she stayed put and glared as if she wanted to eat me. A colossal violence was roiling in me. My hands were shaking. They jerked toward her. Clasping them to control their movements, I said, through clenched jaws, "You wrote a letter, ma'am."

A cold mountain wind came in through the window, nipping at my ears. I felt hot. The door creaked. From time to time, I'd hit the frame irately and it would go on creaking, irritating me, though I never thought to close it. Madalena looked as if she didn't hear anything. "Think you're going to get away with this?" I asked her and a lithograph hanging on the wall.

Marciano's oldest boy entered on tiptoe. Without turning toward him, I shouted, "Go away!"

The child moved toward the window.

"Go away!" I bellowed again. My appearance probably shocked him.

"Closing up the church, Sr. Paulo."

I could tell I sounded out of control, so I made myself say, with a warmth I didn't feel, "Sounds good. Come back later. It's still early."

Nine, on the sacristy clock.

The northeaster started to blow, and the door banged furiously. I buried my hands in my hair. "What are you doing, brat?"

The kid fled.

I don't even know how long I stood there. Rage turned to anguish, anguish to exhaustion.

"Who was the letter to?"

I looked from Madalena to the saints in the oratory. The saints didn't know, and Madalena wasn't answering.

What amazed me was how tranquil she looked. I had arrived boiling mad, ready to kill her. Was I supposed to live with someone who'd do this kind of harm?

But the moment had passed. I'd grown muddled and afraid.

The plaster statues didn't care about my agony. And Madalena looked as unaffected as they were. How could she be so calm?

I had every right to kill her. She was guilty. Why should I let her live? I'd pardon her when she was dead.

My fists clenched and moved toward her, but the spasms were growing weak and sporadic.

"Talk," I blurted hesitantly.

"What for?"

"There's a letter. I need to know, understand?" Taking the page, already wrinkled and dirty, out of my pocket, I handed it to her

Madalena spread it out on the table, examined it, and put it aside. "So?"

"I read it." The candle went out. I lit another and let the match burn down to my fingers. "Say something." There had to be some mistake. Madalena could clear it up if she wanted. My heart pounded desperately. I wanted madly to be convinced of her innocence.

"What for?" murmured Madalena. "For three years, we've

been living a life of horrors. Whenever we try to talk, we end up fighting."

"But the letter?"

Madalena picked up the paper, folded it, and handed it to me. "The rest is in the study, on my desk. This page probably flew out into the garden while I was writing."

"Who's it to?"

"You'll see. It's on top of my desk. There's no reason to be upset. You'll see."

"Fine." I let out a breath, dead tired.

"Will you forgive the unhappiness I've caused you, Paulo?"

"I guess I had my reasons."

"I'm not talking about that. Forgive me?"

I growled a monosyllable.

"Your jealousy wrecked everything, Paulo."

Words of remorse came into my mouth, but stupid pride made me swallow them again. You've got to holler or the herd won't come home.

"Make friends with my aunt, Paulo? When this quarrel is over, you'll see what a good person she is."

I'd been so rough on that poor old lady! "It's because of all this," I said. "Plus it's partly her fault. She's crabby."

"Sr. Ribeiro is an honest worker, don't you think?" Madalena went on.

"Yes, yes. In the olden days, he dealt the cards. Now he's an outcast. He's a decent sort, poor sod."

"And Padilha..."

"No way! He's a schemer. Don't you go pulling for him. The worst sort of reprobate."

"Take it easy! What about Marciano...You're way too strict with Marciano, Paulo."

"Come on," I said, getting riled. "What a litany!"

"Don't be angry," said Madalena without raising her voice.

"What I want..." I sat on a bench. What I wanted was for her to settle my doubts.

"What do you want?" asked Madalena, also sitting down.

"I haven't a clue!" I hunched into myself, my hands heavy on my knees.

Half-serious, half-playful, Madalena said, "If I were to die suddenly—"

"What are you talking about now, woman? That came out of nowhere."

"Why? Who knows when my end might come? If I were to die suddenly—"

"Cut it out! Fiend. What are you going on about?"

"Offer my clothes to Mestre Caetano's family and to Rosa. Share the books out among Sr. Ribeiro, Padilha, and Gondim."

I stood up, impatient. "What a pointless conversation!" I seized on a pleasant topic to drive away the sad ones. "I feel like traveling." Cheered up, I sat down again and lit a cigarette. "After the harvest. I'll leave Sr. Ribeiro in charge of the ranch. Let's go to Bahia. Or better, Rio. We'll rest up for a few months. Your stomach will get better, you'll gain some weight, have fun, get some air. It's not healthy, spending our whole lives in this hole, working like blacks! And we'll make a little hop over to São Paulo. Sound good?"

Madalena watched shadows and light flickering on the wall. She said, "This morning, in the woods, the pau d'arcos were already in bloom, at least four. Beautiful. They'll last a week. Such a shame the flowers fall so quickly."

"Really," I muttered. What connected Rio and São Paulo to the pau d'arcos? "And what about a trip?"

She was staring at the candle. "Yes, I was praying. Not properly. I don't really know how. Never had time to learn."

My God! How her mind wandered. She was answering my first question now.

"I'd write and write till my fingers fell asleep. Tiny letters, to save on paper. Nights before exams, I would sleep two, three hours at most. I had no security, understand? On top of all this, our house on Levada was damp and cold. In winter, I'd bring my books into the kitchen. When could I have gone to church? I was always studying, always, afraid of failing…"

She wasn't right in the mind. I could see perfectly well that she wasn't. She went on speaking incoherently. "The tenant workers' houses, down below, are damp and cold. It's so sad. I was praying for them. For all of you. Praying… I was talking to myself." The clock in the sacristy struck midnight. "My God! So late already. And here I am nattering on." She got up and put her hand on my shoulder. "Goodbye, Paulo. I'm going to go get some rest." She turned toward the door. "Let go of your rage, Paulo."

Why didn't I go with the poor little thing? Who knows? Because I was guarding what was left of my asinine dignity. Because she didn't ask me. Because I was held back by a consuming laziness.

I stayed, ruminating on Madalena's disconnected words and strange manner. Then I remembered the unfinished letter she'd left in the study.

Who was it for? Jealousy filled me again. There was no end to it.

I drowsed, falling little by little into a fitful, troubled sleep. I dreamed, I think, of swamps and swollen rivers.

When I came to, the candle had gone out and the light

of the moon, which I hadn't seen rising, was shining in through the window. The door was still grating. The north-easter shot dry leaves into the sacristy, where they rustled on the black and white paving stones. The clock had stopped, so there was no telling how long I'd slept. Maybe hours. Cocks started crowing, the moon set, the wind got tired of screaming for nothing, and dawn's light played over the images in the oratory.

I stood, my back aching. I stretched my arms, dead tired, feeling like I'd been whipped.

I went out toward the corral, drank a cup of milk, and talked owls for a moment with Marciano. Then I crossed the courtyard, hoping the light of day might make everything clear.

The woods, decorated with pau d'arcos, really were beautiful.

Three years of marriage. That made it exactly a year since this jealous hell started.

The sawmill whistle blew; Sr. Ribeiro's side-whiskers appeared in a window; Maria das Dores opened the doors; Casimiro Lopes showed up with an armful of vegetables.

I went down to the dam, worn out, my hips aching. What a night! I stripped off under the banana trees, dove into the water, and swam.

The sun was already high when I got to the house. My back still ached. What a night!

I was climbing the steps up the path, when I heard horrible screams from inside. "What the hell is this commotion?"

I ran inside, and down the hall on the right to my bedroom. From inside, people were crying out. Pushing them aside, I stopped short. Madalena was stretched out on the bed, white, her eyes glassy, foam at the corners of her mouth.

I went close. Clasped her hands—cold and hard. Put my hand to her heart—stopped. Stopped.

Liquid stained the wood floor under broken glass.

Dona Glória lay collapsed on the rug, sobbing convulsively. The nanny wept, with the child in her arms. Maria das Dores whimpered.

I rubbed Madalena's hands to revive her, stammering, "For God, nothing is impossible." I'd heard that in the field a few days ago. Now it came back, offering some absurd hope.

I held a mirror up to Madalena's mouth and lifted her eyelids. Mechanically, I repeated, "For God, nothing is impossible."

"What a tragedy, Sr. Paulo Honório, what a tragedy!" Sr. Ribeiro murmured nearby.

And Padilha, huddled behind him, said, "In a moment like this, I had no choice but to come."

"I'm grateful, very grateful." I went to the study out of force of habit, all the time murmuring, "For God, nothing is impossible."

On Madalena's desk was the envelope she had told me about. I opened it. It was a long letter saying goodbye to me. I read it, skipping over parts, only understanding sections, tripping constantly on big words I had no way of knowing. One page was missing: the one I had in my wallet, between bills for cement and a spell against malaria that Rosa, years ago, had given me.

32

SHE WAS buried under the high altar's mosaic.

I dressed in black, ordered a headstone. Sr. Magalhães, Padre Silvestre, João Nogueira, Azevedo Gondim, and the neighboring farmers came with condolences. I left the double bed and moved into a small bedroom that had a nest of wrens in the eaves, among the roof tiles. The wrens chirped desperately in the mornings. On the bedside table, telegrams and black-bordered envelopes piled up.

For distraction, I chopped trees in the woods obsessively. Then I arranged repairs on the big leaky wall of the dam.

But my enthusiasm dampened fast. All that was the way of life, not the way of death.

I thought about Madalena. One way or another, thoughts of her were always with me, even if, in the turmoil of those early days, they were mixed in with a bundle of other problems. When those problems sank to dregs in my spirit, though, she rose to the surface. Once in a while, I could stir myself and dissolve her image, but it would quickly come together again and stay there, suspended.

The most interesting subjects made me yawn. I paced around the living room, hands stuck in my pockets, pipe stuck in my mouth. I'd go to the study, browse the books without seeing them, leave, walk down the halls, around the bedrooms, back to the living room.

One day in the garden, I sat watching a large ant executing pointless marches and countermarches. Pointless by my lights, obviously—as though I knew his intentions.

Dona Glória's obnoxious voice interrupted my ruminations. "I came to say goodbye. I'm going away."

I raised my head. She was in front of me, stiff and struggling in her old, ill-fitting dress. It puffed out at the shoulders whenever she stood up straight.

"Where are you off to?"

Dona Glória described a vague arc with her bony finger. "Away."

"You haven't got anywhere to go, ma'am." I looked for the ant, but it had disappeared.

"I'm off," Dona Glória replied firmly.

I tried to talk her out of it. "You're not making sense, woman. Heading off without a place to land? Show some sense."

Dona Glória continued, straight as a broom handle. "I'm not asking advice. I came to bid you goodbye, not flee like an escaped black. Say whatever you want."

I began my endless pacing from one side to another. "Fine. Follow your own nose. When are you coming back?"

"Never."

"Fine, fine." I quickened my pace. "Who are you going with?"

"With God."

"Great, then. The car has a full tank. Enjoy yourself."

"Thank you, but I'm going on foot."

I blew my top. "You're going nowhere!" Panting, I stopped. "Setting off into the world, any which way you want, and saying I threw you out of the house, I'm a cheapskate, you fled without two nickels to rub together. Is that what you're doing?"

Dona Glória was offended, stretching taller with each word. "Are you planning to keep me here, sir? I never killed, never robbed, never slandered. I'm getting out."

I said, "Who said anything about keeping you here? Enough with this lunacy. Want to leave? Go ahead—I don't see you in chains. If you want to stay, though, you could till you're old and ugly, without anyone stepping on your toes. If not, we're done. But it makes no sense at all taking to your heels like someone's driving you out. What the hell. Throwing yourself on God's mercies, lock, stock, and barrel. No. Take some time, prepare, put your things in order."

"They're in order."

"Then travel decently, like a normal person. Figure out where you'll live and how much you need to get by."

"I don't need anything. I don't know where I'll live. All I know is I have to leave today."

"You're acting like a child," I said, dragging out my words. "Could you survive real hardships? There won't be any half measures. Those novels might have spoiled you even for baptism registries."

Little by little, Dona Glória backed down. I didn't know whether she always backed down or whether she'd come with that in mind.

"Consider city rents. Consider the price of medicine. Getting sick is easy, Dona Glória, but it's hard work getting healthy again. Consider groceries, electricity, the water bill. Life is tough everywhere these days, but in the city, Dona Glória, life is the pits."

Dona Glória haughtily admitted that, indeed, life in the city was the pits. She had staunchly stood her ground. It didn't seem fair to keep pushing her.

I said I owed Madalena three years' salary. Dona Glória

believed me, or said she did. "It makes sense for you to be the one to receive it, ma'am."

Dona Glória agreed.

I gave her money to pay for the trip and remitted a pension of two hundred milreis monthly for her to João Nogueira. He would host her for a night, then see her off.

A few days later, Sr. Ribeiro quit.

"Are you serious, Sr. Ribeiro?"

"This house gives rise to bitter memories in me."

"Me too, my man. But you—leaving? What the hell! It's madness."

"Too true, Sr. Paulo Honório, too true."

"Do you have an offer of some work?"

"None at all."

"So? Madness. I can't even recommend you to anyone. Who's going to employ a gentleman of your age? At least, after so many years living here, and so frugally, you're leaving with a fortune. You'll always have enough to get by."

"I will be pining, Sr. Paulo Honório," Sr. Ribeiro whimpered, wiping his eyes. "Pining. It's excruciating. I leave with a broken heart."

"Then don't go, my man! Everyone here likes you. Stay."

"Impossible, entirely impossible. My resolution is immovable."

"Fine." I looked sadly at the study, more spacious since Madalena's desk had been shoved in a corner.

And so the excellent Sr. Ribeiro—who I'd hoped to bury at São Bernardo—ended up drifting from cafés to park benches, carrying his old age and his memories.

33

PADILHA started walking through the courtyard, getting closer to the house and paying me compliments whenever he saw me. One day, he finally came up onto the porch and lingered for an instant. I pretended not to notice these maneuvers.

"Come on in, Padilha."

The month's grace I had given him to withdraw had dribbled away. Padilha came in and stayed. I let him. At least he was company.

Scowling and overcome with laziness, I'd look at the fences of Bom-Sucesso and think about the two Mendonça women living more or less in misery, while Padilha talked. He talked like he was drinking water from a cowbell. I didn't pay attention to anything he said. Nothing. At least it was a human voice. Before long, he'd leave.

One day, Azevedo Gondim brought rumors of revolution. The south had revolted, the center had revolted, the northeast had revolted. "It's the end of the world."

Padilha rubbed his hands. "The boil has finally burst, by God!"

By night, the political authorities had written asking me for arms and fighters. At dawn, I sent them a truck full of rifles and men.

After this, rumors grew into facts: battalions came together, regiments came together, columns formed and were rapidly dispatched, scarlet flags flew everywhere, and the Government of the Republic was corralled in Rio.

"It's a barbarian invasion!" Azevedo Gondim cried. "We're lost!"

Padilha, constantly agitated, devoured manifestos and gnawed his nails. Finally, when the red wave deluged the state, he abruptly disappeared. João Nogueira shed some light on the case: "Padilha and Padre Silvestre joined up with the revolutionary troops and got their orders."

34

SORDID gossip circulated in the city. I kept my distance—never did care for small town intrigue.

It was bitter medicine the way my party had toppled at the first blow. "My turn to eat from the rotten side now. Without a whimper."

Pereira, the Gamas, and Fidélis—they were on the rise and had it in for me. I was getting fed up with all of it. It's not as though they could do anything major: cut the wire fence, send a police delegation to the market, confiscate a farmhand's knife and slap him with his own blade. Predictable.

The worst was that Padilha had lured away some ten or twelve moronic mestizos, who'd enlisted along with him in the revolutionary army. They'd be back.

And for what? That vagabond life, the drills, it'd be better for them.

I yawned a yawn fit to break my jaw. What an idiotic life. True, there was the little boy, but I didn't like him—so delicate, so pale.

If he bucked up a little, I might bring him to the sawmill. If he grew up sickly as he was, better to educate him.

Plans were made. "To hell with plans." The world around me was rapidly becoming a maelstrom of horrors. And the wider world was chaos, demonic confusion, an even bigger maelstrom.

Friends at the newspapers kept me posted on the revolution. "Damnation!" Azevedo Gondim cried. "It was a bluff. Threats by telegraph and radio, flyers tossed from airplanes—everyone coming apart with fear. The most cowardly people God ever created."

"That's an exaggeration," the lawyer opined. "They were brave."

"Brave how?" Gondim bellowed. "Folks who should have fought hid instead."

"Those on the side of the old state. The revolutionaries are different—they're idealistic, courageous. I wouldn't say any of this in public, but they are."

"The devil can take their idealism. And as for their courage—"

"Let's be fair, Gondim," I intervened, soothing, mild. "This was in the lifeblood of the people. It wasn't worth fighting."

"Wasn't worth it! Now it wasn't worth it! Everyone thought that way, so they came on in. And so brazen! Government bigwigs appearing suddenly with red scarves at their necks."

"That was in Alagoas," João Nogueira interrupted.

"It was everywhere, man. Even now, lots don't cross over because they'd be rejected."

"As far as I'm concerned," Nogueira declared, "it suits me fine to be on top or on the bottom because politics does nothing for me. I've hit bottom and I see no prospects for rising. It's true that I always thought democracy made no sense. I've said it to you before. The hell of it is I voted for the government slate. But between us, the only reason the dictatorship doesn't work is that we're flat on our backs."

Gondim protested, getting indignant.

I said, "All I want is to see Padre Silvestre in a lieutenant's uniform."

"What does he get out of playing the patriot?" said Nogueira.

"Animal!" growled Azevedo Gondim. The *Cruzeiro* had lost its subsidy.

Conversations like this distracted me. Once a week, the two of them had supper with me. Some city fanatics started rumors that São Bernardo was a nest of reactionaries.

"How goes the fight?"

"Badly."

News arrived: gratuitous violence, revenge, commissions of inquiry airing dirty laundry.

Nogueira, a moderate, wanted an accord between victors and defeated.

Gondim detested accords. A tooth for a tooth—get it? He advocated violence to me, to Nogueira, to the trees in the orchard, trying to get us fomenting a counterrevolution (the quicker the better) to drive out this mob of impostors. He wanted vigorous government, yessir, tough, yessir, but sensible, a working government that would reestablish order and creditor confidence and the *Cruzeiro*'s monthly subsidy of a hundred and fifty milreis. We couldn't go on this way.

He spouted big fat words, all-purpose words from the newspaper. São Paulo had to rise up boldly; in São Paulo, a sacred flame would blaze; from São Paulo, the land of flag-bearing pioneers, new flag-bearers would emerge and win back the freedom we had cast aside.

"You speak well, Gondim," I'd murmur, impressed. "I'm sure you'd be on the rise if our party weren't on its back with its legs in the air."

João Nogueira criticized the election and exerted influence

over the advisory councils. Gondim treasured the vote as if it were a small child. He thought the only place for advisers was in parliamentary commissions. Casimiro Lopes listened in wonder from a distance.

I gazed at the church tower, my thoughts reaching out through the landscape, pulling back again, wandering down the stairs, through the garden and the orchard and on into the sacristy.

João Nogueira was condemning revolutionary literature, counterfeit patriotism.

The oratory, above the table, was full of saints. Lithographs hung on the wall. The door banged on its hinges and the candle went out. I lit another and let the match burn down to my fingers. The workers' houses were cold and damp. Mestre Caetano's family was living in pitiful poverty. And poor Marciano, so worn out, hollowed out, laid so low!

Azevedo Gondim was shouting, proclaiming liberty. He contented himself with the paltry proceeds from his rag, up to his ears in debt. He's adjusted to this. What he wants is to see the newspaper foaming at the mouth with its sleeves rolled up. And to insult the half-wit politicians, in Sousa's pool hall, when the red ball doesn't drop.

The candle had gone out. It was late. The door creaked. Moonlight came in through the window. The northeaster scattered leaves on the floor, and I wasn't hearing Gondim's bellows anymore.

35

I STARTED the new year on the wrong foot. Various clients I'd long done business with suddenly went broke. Some fled. There were suicides. The *Daily Notices* bulged with bankruptcies and forced liquidations. I made do with the worst settlements.

As a result, I let the beekeeping, vegetable gardening, and orchard-keeping go. The oranges ripened and rotted on their stems. We left them. It was either that or pick, sort, wrap, and ship them more or less for free.

Bad luck never comes alone. The clothing factories used to advance money for cotton, but they suddenly reversed this excellent policy, so much so they started buying on credit. I sold one harvest on the spindle this way, and worse: they cheated me on the classification.

The cotton gin and the sawmill needed new machinery, but at a point when it would have added up to a fortune—the dollar was sky-high.

"No more games. Why should I sacrifice myself and end up delivering the merchandise for free just to kiss these crooks' hands?"

On top of all this, the banks shut their doors to me. I don't know why, but they did. It's not like I was ever late on my payments. One bad break after another. Pushed to the edge, I told off a manager. "Look, if you gentlemen won't come to an agreement, just say so. Either these papers have value or they don't. If they do, hand over the dough. Cheats! Did I ask for a revolution?"

In six months, everyone was so broke that I sold the car for a song to keep them from coming after me for a stray promissory note of six contos.

"Ebb tide. Now the lazy ones are winning. Mendonça should have lived, with his scrub-covered property and dead factory. Work is for ants. I'm throwing in the towel."

And I threw in the towel.

One day, towel thrown, I was sadly contemplating the cotton gin and the sawmill. João Nogueira came with the news that Fidélis and the Gamas were questioning the property lines again. The worst part was that Sr. Magalhães had moved to another district.

"The wonders of revolution," Nogueira commented. "An immovable civil servant! A decent judge like Magalhães! A judge with integrity!"

I shrugged my shoulders, disheartened. João Nogueira was also disheartened. Nothing to be done.

I started mechanically pacing through the house again. From time to time, I'd push open the study door to give Sr. Ribeiro an order. I thought I saw Dona Glória fooling around in the orchard, holding a novel. And my pacing took me to the bedrooms, as if I were looking for someone.

36

It's been two years since Madalena died, two hard years. But when friends stopped coming to discuss politics, it became unbearable.

Which was how I got the strange idea of putting this story together with help from people who know more than I do. The idea flopped, as I've already said. About four months ago, though, while writing to a certain fellow in Minas, turning down some confusing trade of pork for zebu cattle, I heard an owl hoot and sat up in alarm.

I had to send Marciano up the church tower the next day.

All of a sudden, the idea of creating this book came back to me. I signed the letter to the pork man and, after wavering for an instant, not knowing how to start something like this, I drafted a chapter.

Since then I've done my best to husk the facts, sitting here at the dining room table, smoking my pipe and drinking coffee until the crickets chirp and the orange leaves are tinged with shadow.

Sometimes I go straight until night, passing endless time awakening memories. Other times, I can't settle into this new kind of work.

For example, yesterday and the day before were a total loss. I tried uselessly to channel these words pouring down like mountain rains toward some reasonable conclusion, but what appeared before me was a massive disgust. Disgust and vague awareness of feelings, many feelings.

I am a destroyed man. Sick? No. I'm in perfect health. When Costa Brito vomited out those two articles, after he couldn't shake me down for those two hundred milreis, he called me sick, alluding to crimes imputed to me. Brito: what an ass. Up until today, by God's grace, a doctor has never entered my house. I've never been sick, not once.

What I am is old. Fifty years on São Pedro's day. Fifty lost years, fifty years senselessly squandered, mistreating myself and mistreating others, with the result that I've grown hard, so callous that no scratch could penetrate this thick hide and hurt the blunted soul inside.

Fifty years! So many useless hours! A person can use up his whole life without knowing what for! Eating and sleeping like a pig. Like a pig! Getting up early each morning, trotting out in search of food, just to keep the food for the children, grandchildren, and all the generations after. Idiocy! Hogwash! Wouldn't it be better for the devil to take it all?

Sun, rain, sleepless nights, calculations, combinations, violence, dangers—and I'm not even left with the illusion of having done anything much. The garden, the vegetable patch, the orchard—abandoned. Peking ducks—dead. Cotton, castor beans—drying up. And my neighbors' fences, my ferocious enemies, encroach.

Obviously, after the crisis ends, the property could be rebuilt and returned to what it was. The field hands would exhaust themselves, working from sunup to sundown, fed on manioc meal and cod fins. Trucks would roll again, transporting merchandise to the railroad. The ranch would fill once more with movement and noise.

But what for? What for? Won't you all tell me? There

would be so much weeping amidst this movement and this noise. There would be so much despair. The little children, in their cold, damp huts, would be swollen with worms. And Madalena would not be here to send them medicine and milk. Men and women are sad creatures.

Animals—the creatures who'd served me all these years were animals. There were domestic animals, such as Padilha; wild animals, such as Casimiro Lopes; and tame animals, oxen, who worked the fields. The corrals, propped against each other down below, had electric lights. The stoutest calves spelled with a primer and learned the Ten Commandments by heart.

Animals. Some switched species and joined the army, turning left, turning right, standing guard. Others sought greener pastures.

If I filled the corrals, I'd have good harvests, deposit money in the banks, buy more land, and construct more corrals. What for? When would I ever be content?

I'd placed myself above my class. To my mind, I raised myself up. As I said, I'd been a blind man's guide, a sweetseller, and a field hand. I'm positive not a single one of those jobs gave me the brains it took to create this narrative. It's nothing much, I agree, but in my brighter moments, I reckon that what I hold in my hands is in some ways better than Gondim's literature. Anyway, I'm far superior to Mestre Caetano and his ilk, even if my soul's vestments aren't much more than tatters of knowledge, gathered without schooling and badly sewn. I don't have a problem admitting it's a shabby superiority that makes me so vain.

Apart from this, I don't think the mercantile writing and manuals on agriculture and animal husbandry that gave me my basic education made me a better person than when I plowed a rut. At least back then I never dreamed of being the ferocious exploiter I became.

As far as the rest of the benefits—houses, lands, furniture, livestock, political favors, etc.—I have to agree these are little but external trappings.

I think I took a wrong turn somewhere.

If I'd continued scouring old Margarida's copper pan, she and I would have led a quiet life. We'd have talked little and thought less. At night, on her mat, after coffee with raw sugar, we would have prayed African prayers in God's good graces.

If I hadn't wounded João Fagundes, I might have married Germana. I'd own a half-dozen horses and a little plot of hay, some oilcloths and wooden yokes. I'd be a passable mule driver. I'd have credit on the ranch, good for a hundred milreis in the city's shops. My wife and children would have new clothes on each of the four annual festivals. My wants would circle a narrow orbit. No unnecessary worries would torment me. I'd be pleasant. And on winter mornings, driving my mule train, cracking my *buranhém* stick, wearing sandals and an *ouricuri* hat, with a few nickels in my purse, I'd swallow a gulp of cane liquor to chase off the cold and sing to these roads, happy as the damned.

Today I don't sing or laugh. If I see myself in a mirror, I'm upset by my own hard mouth and hard eyes.

I think of the village where Sr. Ribeiro lived, half a century ago. Sr. Ribeiro earned, yes, but not for himself. He had a big house, always full, and *caboclo* pumpkins rotting in the fields. Within his territory, no one went hungry. What if I lived in the time of the monarchy, under Sr. Ribeiro's protection? I don't know how to read. I don't know anything about electric lights or telephones. When I try to express myself,

I talk in circles and gesticulate a lot. Like everyone, I have an oil lamp for no reason, since we all sleep at night. A hundred revolutions could break out and I wouldn't even hear about them. In all likelihood, I'm a happy fellow.

With a shudder, I abandon this happiness that isn't mine to find myself here in São Bernardo, writing.

The windows are closed. It's midnight, not a sound in the deserted house.

I get up to search for a candle, since the light's about to go out. I'm not sleepy. To lie down, toss on the pillows until dawn—torture. I prefer to sit up, to finish this. Tomorrow holds no charm for me.

I put the candle in the holder, strike a match, light it. I shiver. Madalena's memory stalks me. Trying to pull away from it, I circle the table, squeezing my hands till my nails pierce the skin. When I come to, I'm biting my lips to the point of drawing blood.

After a long, long while, weary, I write one line. I say in a low voice, "I wrecked my life. I wrecked it stupidly." My agitation lessens. "I stupidly wrecked my life."

I force myself to think about Madalena. If it were possible to start over . . . What am I fooling myself for? If it were possible to start over, what would happen is exactly what happened. I haven't managed to change, and this is what makes me feel the worst.

Mestre Caetano's urchins drag themselves around out there, soiled, starving. Rosa, her belly broken from so many births, works in the house, works in the fields, and works in the bed. Her husband is more of a milksop all the time. And the remaining tenant farmers are as backward as he is.

Honestly, those wretches don't move me. I pity them and acknowledge my role in their situation, but I won't go beyond that. There's such a distance between us! We were all together at first, but this damned way of life separated us.

Madalena entered here full of good thoughts and good intentions, but those thoughts and intentions collided with my cruelty and selfishness.

I wasn't always selfish and cruel, or so I believe. My way of life made me bad. The terrible suspicion, pointing out enemies everywhere! This way of making a living made me useless. It crippled me. I bet I have a tiny heart, gaps in the brain, nerves different from other men's. Not to mention an enormous nose, enormous mouth, and enormous fingers.

If this is how Madalena saw me, she must have found me unbelievably ugly.

Closing my eyes, I shake my head to drive away the vision of these monstrous deformities.

The candle is nearly out.

I think my mind wandered. I hallucinated swamps, swollen rivers, the figure of a werewolf. Outside, a great silence looms in devilish darkness.

Meantime, moonlight enters through the closed window, and the furious northeaster scatters dry leaves on the floor.

Horrible! If only someone would appear...but they're all sleeping.

If at least the child would cry...I could never even feel any affection for my child. What misery!

Casimiro Lopes is sleeping. Marciano is sleeping. Curs!

I'll stay here in the gloom until I don't know when, until, dead tired, I lean my head on the table to take a few minutes' rest.

TRANSLATOR'S NOTE

SÃO BERNARDO is the story of Paulo Honório, a former field hand who buys and restores the property where he was once a field hand. The book is premised, in other words, on a dramatic irony. Smaller ironies thread it throughout. Sr. Paulo learns to read only as an adult, as a result of a stint in jail. After the tragic loss of his wife and a serious downturn in his fortunes, he writes a memoir, which he titles *São Bernardo*, the name of his property. At various points in the book, he recounts conversations in which he has disparaged literature and literary pursuits. Speaking to us from bourgeois salons, surrounded by readers of novels, he casts himself, by contrast, as a truth-teller.

Sr. Paulo writes in his own rough-hewn voice—exclamatory, spontaneous, colorful. The argot is so specific to the book's region and epoch, in fact, that there is a published guide to interpreting expressions found in this novel, *Glossário Regional/Popular da Obra São Bernardo, de Graciliano Ramos*, by Maria da Salete Figueiredo de Carvalho and Maria das Neves Alcântara de Pontes. The authors' sources were mostly dictionaries and other lexical studies of the Brazilian northeast, but still, some of Sr. Paulo's expressions are *não dicionarizada*—not found in any of the hundred-odd print sources the authors have listed.

These facets of the book—irony, illiteracy, and idiomatic

obscurity—shaped my idea of what it meant to be faithful to it. Where it was tempting to smooth a jagged transition or an awkward sentence, I tried to preserve its roughness or strangeness if those qualities were present in the original. Most educated Brazilians—the class Sr. Paulo is writing for but not the class from which he comes—would not be familiar with most of the expressions in the book. This was vividly reinforced when I was consulting with a Brazilian friend, a brilliant and determined interlocutor, who was stumped by many of the expressions. Finally, in a flash of insight, she said that she believed that Graciliano Ramos possibly intended for readers occasionally to feel thwarted by Sr. Paulo's way of talking. "Graciliano is a demon!" she shouted. "I love him!"

I didn't need to speculate on Ramos's intentions to recognize that her analysis made perfect sense. This is the story, after all, of a man in a unique and lonely position, a position he reflects on at his own story's close—how, had he remained illiterate, he might not have been estranged both from his own kind and from himself. He has never tried to gain entrance into the bourgeois world; he doesn't crave it and knows it is blocked to him. It's the book's other great irony, of course, that Sr. Paulo's successes made his life impossible. His story, told in the language of the class he has left behind for the benefit of the class he cannot fully join, functions as a metonym for this impossible situation.

So if an expression is strange to Brazilians, I often translated it literally in order to maintain its strangeness, whereas if it is a common expression in Brazilian Portuguese but strange to us, I usually rendered it as a common North American idiom. I also tried in other ways to replicate the linguistic breadth of the book. Various Brazilian critics have written on repetition and lexical choices in Ramos's novels, and the ways these convey the modes of speech and thought of the region where his novels are set. *São Bernardo*, told in the first person by a man who fancies himself a writer, is admittedly more colorful, say, than *Vidas Secas* (*Barren Lives*, 1938), a third-person story about taciturn and illiterate farmhands. Still, I tracked the incidence of many words, in hopes of roughly replicating their frequency. Especially where repetitions came in rapid succession, I tried my best to reproduce them.

Much of *São Bernardo*'s genius, I think, is in the ways that Sr. Paulo's actions, attitudes, and language lure us into uncomfortable regions of simultaneous sympathy and dis-identification. To soften his linguistic edges in the interest of making the book more accessible would be to dull the book's light—its humor, ironic self-awareness, and linguistic sophistication. I thought this particularly important because it seems that Ramos was ardently exact in his writing. As the American critic Fred P. Ellison notes: "We have reason to suspect that the choice of an adjective may have caused Ramos 'to sweat in agony,' as has been said of Flaubert.... With Ramos, language is a precision tool with which effects hitherto unrecorded in Brazilian literature have been made." He quotes Guilherme Figueiredo, marveling on similar matters: "The constant polishing of his style ... lends almost astounding force to a mere sentence, to a mere word ... his expressions are immutable in their framework."

Rachel de Queiroz, a contemporary, praised Ramos's "vaguely brilliant quick tone." It has been an honor to bask in that brilliance and to try to turn its glow toward English readers.

—P.V.

TITLES IN SERIES

For a complete list of titles, visit www.nyrb.com or write to:
Catalog Requests, NYRB, 435 Hudson Street, New York, NY 10014

GRACILIANO RAMOS São Bernardo
FRIEDRICH RECK Diary of a Man in Despair
JULES RENARD Nature Stories
JEAN RENOIR Renoir, My Father
GREGOR VON REZZORI Abel and Cain
GREGOR VON REZZORI An Ermine in Czernopol
GREGOR VON REZZORI Memoirs of an Anti-Semite
GREGOR VON REZZORI The Snows of Yesteryear: Portraits for an Autobiography
JULIO RAMÓN RIBEYRO The Word of the Speechless: Selected Stories
TIM ROBINSON Stones of Aran: Labyrinth
TIM ROBINSON Stones of Aran: Pilgrimage
MILTON ROKEACH The Three Christs of Ypsilanti
FR. ROLFE Hadrian the Seventh
GILLIAN ROSE Love's Work
LINDA ROSENKRANTZ Talk
LILLIAN ROSS Picture
WILLIAM ROUGHEAD Classic Crimes
CONSTANCE ROURKE American Humor: A Study of the National Character
SAKI The Unrest-Cure and Other Stories; illustrated by Edward Gorey
UMBERTO SABA Ernesto
JOAN SALES Uncertain Glory
TAYEB SALIH Season of Migration to the North
TAYEB SALIH The Wedding of Zein
JEAN-PAUL SARTRE We Have Only This Life to Live: Selected Essays. 1939–1975
ARTHUR SCHNITZLER Late Fame
GERSHOM SCHOLEM Walter Benjamin: The Story of a Friendship
DANIEL PAUL SCHREBER Memoirs of My Nervous Illness
JAMES SCHUYLER Alfred and Guinevere
JAMES SCHUYLER What's for Dinner?
SIMONE SCHWARZ-BART The Bridge of Beyond
LEONARDO SCIASCIA The Day of the Owl
LEONARDO SCIASCIA Equal Danger
LEONARDO SCIASCIA The Moro Affair
LEONARDO SCIASCIA To Each His Own
LEONARDO SCIASCIA The Wine-Dark Sea
VICTOR SEGALEN René Leys
ANNA SEGHERS The Seventh Cross
ANNA SEGHERS Transit
PHILIPE-PAUL DE SÉGUR Defeat: Napoleon's Russian Campaign
GILBERT SELDES The Stammering Century
VICTOR SERGE The Case of Comrade Tulayev
VICTOR SERGE Conquered City
VICTOR SERGE Memoirs of a Revolutionary
VICTOR SERGE Midnight in the Century
VICTOR SERGE Notebooks, 1936–1947
VICTOR SERGE Unforgiving Years
VARLAM SHALAMOV Kolyma Stories
VARLAM SHALAMOV Sketches of the Criminal World: Further Kolyma Stories
SHCHEDRIN The Golovlyov Family
ROBERT SHECKLEY Store of the Worlds: The Stories of Robert Sheckley
CHARLES SIMIC Dime-Store Alchemy: The Art of Joseph Cornell
MAY SINCLAIR Mary Olivier: A Life
WILLIAM SLOANE The Rim of Morning: Two Tales of Cosmic Horror